P
JAIMIE ENGLE

"…the world Engle has created in this novel is an intriguing one, equal parts familiar and fantastic." *Kirkus Reviews*

"…belongs on your bookshelf - young or old - right along with Tolkien and Grimm." –5-Star Review

"I did not want to leave until the last page was turned." –Kid Lit Reviews

"…the same kind of universe you might meet Captain Malcolm Reynolds or Luke Skywalker in." –The Story Sanctuary Reviews

"…a dazzling, fresh plot." –5-Star Review

"A tale presents troubled adolescence and romance through the eyes of a remarkable teen protagonist." –Kirkus Editor's Choice & Review

"Metal Mouth is a brilliantly original tale that explores many concerns countless people deal with every day…" –Reader's Choice Review

"…a wry and wise romantic heartbreaker touched with mystery, lightning, and shivery hints of the supernatural." –Book Life Prize

"…explained and explored thoroughly… structure and development is very well executed" –Book Life Prize Non-Fiction

BOOKS BY JAIMIE ENGLE
FICTION

Clifton Chase and the Arrow of Light, Book 1
One boy is chosen to change history

Clifton Chase and the Arrow of Light, Coloring Book
Condensed version of the novel with pictures to color

Clifton Chase on Castle Rock, Book 2
The adventure continues, only this time it's with Robin Hood

Clifton Chase on Castle Rock, Coloring Book 2
Condensed version of book two with pictures to color

The Dredge
Supernatural gifts are sought through deception in a future world

Dreadlands: Wolf Moon
A Viking boy must face shifting wolves or become their prey

The Toilet Papers: Places to Go, while you Go
Short story collection of humor, horror, and historical for adults 16+

The Toilet Papers, Jr.
Short story collection of humor, horror, & fairy tales for kids 8-12

Metal Mouth
A girl's braces transmit a boy's voice after she's struck by lightning

NON-FICTION

Clifton Chase and the Arrow of Light Teacher Guide
Teacher Curriculum Guide to use with the novel

Write a Book that Doesn't Suck (Indie Series Book #2)
A No-Nonsense Guide to Writing Epic Fiction

How to Publish Your Book (Indie Series Book #1)
A step-by-step eBook to get your book published!

Visit the author at JaimieEngle.com

METAL MOUTH

Jaimie Engle

JME Books

Text copyright © 2018 Jaimie Engle
Cover design © 2018 Philip Benjamin of Benjamin Studios
Cover Art by Joshua Menendez
The text for this book is set in Fairfield LT Std Light
All rights reserved, including the right of reproduction in whole or in
part in any form.

Published in the United States by JME Books,
a division of The Write Engle, LLC,
P.O. Box 411242 Melbourne, FL 32941.

Visit us on the Web: JaimieEngle.com

For an author visit or bulk order discounts, visit us at JaimieEngle.com
or email publicity@thewriteengle.com

Summary: A girl's braces begin to transmit a boy's voice in her
head after a near-death experience.

ISBN: 978-1-7328786-0-0
ISBN: 1732878609

10 9 8 7 6 5 4 3 2

Sparking Wonder & Discovery
JME Books

To Christine.

Jaimie Engle

PART ONE

The Gift

▫▫ DR. ANT KILLER ▫▫

Whoever's idea it was to affix metal wires to a person's teeth to straighten them is the same person who burned ants with a magnifying glass as a kid. I'm sure of it. I mean, if God wanted me to have perfectly straight teeth, I think He has the power to make that happen. But no. Some guy with store-bought teeth straps kids like me to cracked-vinyl seats as he clamps wires and brackets into our pried-open mouths and gets his kicks off.

Hello? This is still America, isn't it?

But it gets worse. To really straighten my smile, Dr. Ant Killer regularly tightens these prison bars over my incarcerated teeth. And that's where I sit today, on the cracked chair, like a circus contortionist desperate to get out of harm's way.

"So, Mahlorie, how is school this year?"

"Doin' good," I say, although it comes out as, "'oin' 'ood."

"Good, good," Dr. Ant Killer says, as he wrenches his pliers across my brackets.

I have to wonder if dentists are required to take

Braces as a Second Language in dentistry school. Maybe they sit in a roomful of patients with pried-open mouths who recite Shakespeare and talk politics until they understand them, because if they can decode that, they should have no problem to decipher the daily life of a teenager like me.

"'ow 'uch 'onger?" I ask.

"I'm on the last one, Mahlorie. Not long at all."

Thank God!

"There we go. All finished."

My cheeks are set free and I rub until I can feel them. At the door, Dr. Ant Killer turns and says, "Take it easy today, all right?"

I nod as he flashes his porcelain smile and disappears from the room, ready to torture his next victim. My teeth hurt, and my jaw is sore. I hate this. What does it matter what my teeth look like anyway? Will I get into a better college or make more money if my mouth looks like a white picket fence? I close my eyes and big tears fall down my cheeks.

"Mahlorie?"

Eyes open. Mom stands in the doorway, blonde hair pulled back in a serious bun, crimson-stained lips spread in a sympathetic smile. "You ready to go?"

I nod.

"Milkshake time?" I nod quicker.

If any good can come from a visit with Dr. Ant Killer, it's handmade mint chocolate chip milkshakes from *DiBella's Ice Cream Parlor* and a free day from school to hang with Mom. You may have heard of her, Victoria M. Reddish. She's a famous author who writes

romance novels, "smut books" as my best friend Shai's mom calls them. My mom travels for book signings and to talk at book clubs, but she almost always finds a way to get home on the days I have my braces tightened.

When I was younger, I snuck into Mom's study to read one. I was curious, you know, as a little kid. The title was about different colors with this very cool cover that reminded me of a superhero novel, like the Crimson Avenger or Gillian Gray. Looked cool, so I opened to a random page and read about some quivers and shivers, and I thought maybe the girl needed a blanket. That's not so bad. *Still waters. Calm waters.* Sounded tranquil to me. Then, the book went into this anatomy lesson and before I finished the paragraph I slammed it closed and bolted out of the room with one thought: *I will never, ever fall in love.*

Mom and I pile into her Ford Explorer where, right away, she gets a call from her agent. *Book signing in Chicago? No problem. Conference in Montreal next spring? You bet.* Out the window, the world darkens to an eerie gray that blots out the sun. Fat raindrops plop and bounce on the windshield and hood, until the whole sky opens, and sheets of rain blanket the world in a wet, soggy hug.

So much for milkshakes. Mom would never get her suede pumps wet.

At best, I'll find a yogurt pop in the freezer and watch *The Hunger Games* for the bazillionth time. Mom's chatter dulls into white noise and I fall to sleep.

ooooo

I'm startled awake as the garage door screeches closed. "We're home," Mom says.

I drag myself out of the car, into the house, and upstairs to my bedroom.

"Sorry about the shakes, lambkin," Mom calls. "We can try after supper."

"Sure, Mom." I know good and well that ain't gonna happen. Sometimes, I think Mom cares more about the characters in her books than about me. Maybe I could write myself into one of her novels...

As Raphael reaches for Claudia in a tight embrace, he is pushed aside by Mahlorie Moore, who rescues Claudia from the wretched—although very muscular— arms of her assailant before she Judo-chops him in the neck and heads out for a milkshake with her mom and new best friend, Dia.

A smile tugs one side of my mouth. Not bad work, if I do say so myself. I flop onto my bed and rescue my abandoned cell phone from its charger. Seven missed calls, twelve texts, and more Snaps than I'll ever get to. I check my texts first. Nine are from Shai:

Where U at? What's ↑?
Dr. Ant killer ☻? Sooooo bored.... U OK?
OMG! Rain!! U home yet?
Mr. Skinner's the worst. I miss you. Call me!!!

Shai is the best. We've been friends since the fourth grade when I moved to Melbourne, though we couldn't be more opposite. Shai is a cheerleader, in student government and loves how she's popular. She crushes on every boy in the universe who is cute, blond, and plays sports.

I write for the school newspaper, love musicals, and couldn't care less about fashion or boys or popularity. It's not that people don't like me. It's that I don't care so much. It all seems so shallow to judge a person by the fashion designer whose clothes were mass-produced in a third-world country sweat shop and can only be afforded by parents who have the money

6

to buy them for their spoiled kids.

Shai sees it as art.

I told you, complete opposites.

After one ring, I say, "Hey, Shai. What are you up to?"

"Not a thing. I am so bored! How was Dr. Ant Killer? Still gorgeous?"

"Sure, but he sucks. He made my braces so tight it hurts to talk."

"I'm so sorry, sweetie. You listen then, and I'll catch you up on what you missed. You remember Josh, right?"

I squint in thought. "From science?"

"No. That's Ash. Josh has messy, dirty-blond hair and a smile that makes my body go numb."

"Okay," I say, with a smirk. "What about him?"

"Well Ezra told Jessica who told Olivia and Julia, which was overheard by Nick that Josh and Allie broke up!"

I pause. "So?"

"So? He's single." Shai sighs through the speaker. "I love you, Mal, but sometimes, I don't get you."

"I'm sorry if I don't go nuts over a game of telephone." I'm irritated. I can hear it in my own voice.

"You know I don't see what the big deal is over everyone's status."

"It's not that, Mal. You're so…anti. Don't you ever daydream about that perfect guy who wants you to find him?"

"No. I'm not a nutcase. People actually do that?"

"Maybe that perfect guy dreams of you and

7

doesn't want to wait anymore. Ever think of that? That he will come find you first?"

I laugh. "Great, Shai. That's exactly what I need. A stalker."

"I wouldn't mind so much," Shai says. "If he was cute. But hey, I'll let you go. Feel better, hon. Love you."

"Love you, too."

I stare at the popcorn ceiling for a while and think about what Shai said. *I'm not anti, am I?* Because I don't buy the buzz? Reality television and YouTube sensations. Well, some of them deserve it. But mostly, it's a stupid popularity contest with mindless lookers at the top of the hollow totem pole. That's why I wear these stupid braces. To look better. To conform. To fit society's mold.

Who gives a crap?

But a still small voice inside my head whispers, "You do."

▫▫ INVITATION ▫▫

First period Algebra has got to be the worst way to start the day. Besides the fact that I will never, ever use this information in my day-to-day life, my teacher Ms. Lichtin, seems to think that math is a word that should be spoken with reverence and math facts are the Holy Grail of life. I think it's obscene, and math is a four- letter word.

Today, she's on her A-game. Formulas spew from her mouth like they're part of a Harry Potter spell while the fumes from the markers send us all into oblivion. "Mahlorie?" she squawks. "What is the solution and why?"

I hobble to the board, head lowered. Did she skip ninth grade? I would never humiliate a student for my own pleasure. It should be mandatory grounds for dismissal. I reach the whiteboard and reread the question as if hieroglyphs on an ancient pyramid. My teeth ache into a headache and I'm starved because I don't finish a bagel when it takes forty-five minutes to chew. And it's only first period?

"Mahlorie, I won't wait all day," the teacher is

quick to remind me.

With no answer in sight, I scribble >6 with a marker and beeline back to my seat.

"That is incorrect. Stephen Gonzales. Let's see if you've paid attention."

Hunched forward, Stephen hobbles to the board. Someone should report this teacher for abuse. Ms. Lichtin chooses a few more students for the firing squad, before Marissa Ray answers correctly. Figures. She had her hand up the whole time. I pretend to pay attention for the rest of class, until the bell rings and I am finally released.

"Hey, Mal." Shai walks up, hair split into pigtails tagged with bright ribbons. Knee-high boots and a white button-down somehow match when she wears them. I have to smile at her fearless style. "How was Algebra?" she asks.

"How do you think?" I open my locker and switch out books. "I'd rather have my braces tightened in Dr. Ant Killer's office."

"Couldn't be any worse than Mr. Carmine's World History. We actually watched a video on the manorial system and serfdom."

I stare at Shai. "And?"

She sighs. "And...it was boring. No tension. Only laws and rules and systems. He could've showed us *Braveheart* instead. We would've gotten it."

I smile. "Great film, but wrong system. Feudalism, not manorial."

She ribs me. "You are such a nerd."

"Why? Because I like historically accurate fiction? You know how bent out of shape you get when someone mistakes a knockoff for a designer."

"That is not the same," Shai says, as I close my locker and we push down the crowded hall. "So, I was thinking after school maybe your mom could drop us at the Avenue to walk around. Catch a movie?"

"She left this morning for a weekend conference in Miami."

"Oh. How about your dad? Is he busy?"

"On a cruise, working."

"So, who's gonna stay with you while they're gone?"

"Mrs. Cardillo."

"Mrs. Cardillo? The wino? Oh my God, you are so lucky. She'll be passed out by seven o'clock."

"She's not a wino."

"You're coming with me to a party tonight."

"No, I'm not. I'm going to put on my sweats and do absolutely nada. Maybe download *Braveheart*." Shai doesn't catch my joke.

"But you have to. There's a party tonight for Lucas Chambers. He's gonna make Varsity. I have to be there."

"So be there but leave me out of it. You know I don't like parties. Too much drinking and stupidity in one room. Makes me nervous."

Shai stops, grabs my hand. "Come on, Mal. It's always more fun when you're there. And you know you always have a good time too, once you finally stop moping and start mingling." We reach my second period class. "Not even for a little bit? Everyone will be there. If it sucks, we can leave. I promise. Please?"

I know I will never win an argument with Shai, so I let out a heavy breath of concession. "Fine. But I will hold you to that."

Her eyes sparkle. "You are the greatest best friend in the whole world," Shai says with a hug. "This is gonna be so fun! I promise it'll be a night you won't forget."

That's exactly what I'm afraid of.

"Meet me at your side gate at 9:30. And wear something cute." She glances at my torn jeans and *Back to the Future* tank top. "Better yet, I'll grab you something from my locker."

A wave of nervous excitement builds as I think about the party. I tell myself it will be fun, and I'm sure it will. Shai is always a blast to be around, it's everyone else I worry about. The warning bell rings.

Shai is halfway down the hall. Night Stevenson bounces beside her as I step into chemistry lab. Beakers line the back station. Half the students already wear gaudy goggles. From my peripheral, light flashes as the inside a beaker ignites and bursts through the glass that shatters with a loud crash. A shard sails past but doesn't nick me.

Mrs. Maraschino giggles. "Lucky girl. And that, class, is why you should always wear protective gear when you conduct an experiment. Even you, Miss Moore."

My jaw literally drops. I just walked into the room. I still hold my books, and she shifts blame from her explosion to my improper eye protection? I should sue her for negligence. My classmates laugh at my expense as humiliation warms my cheeks. I can't believe it's only second period. I slam my books on my desk and quickly don my goggles and lab coat before I'm the victim of another fly-by sharding. I know Mrs. Maraschino is certifiable, so as much as I'd like to take her down, I honestly would fear for my life afterward. Probably have to live in protective custody under a false name. I could go by Claudia. I snort a laugh.

"Something funny, Miss Moore?" Mrs. Maraschino asks.

"No, ma'am." I skirt to my place at the lab table. Rumor has it that Mrs. Maraschino never married. Her fiancé supposedly left her at the altar and had his best man hand her a note to call it off because they had bad chemistry. Seriously, I couldn't make this stuff up. People say that she's on a mission to discover exactly what went wrong, and she uses her students to conduct questionable experiments as she searches for the perfect balance.

Or so the gossip goes.

I'm not one to put too much faith into people's words. Talk is cheap, right? Sticks and stones, and all. But really, I think people are plain mean when you get down to it.

"You okay, Mahlorie?"

I turn. Spencer Levine avoids my gaze, but I know he was the one who asked. He's four feet, eleven inches tall, which makes him the shortest freshman in school, and lots of people make it their mission to remind him of that every day.

"Yeah, I'm cool, Spencer."

He walks off without a word. It makes me wonder how much is his personality and how much is the personality he's created to cope with high school bullies. I mean, he doesn't fit the mold, so he doesn't fit in, right? Isn't that how it works? Sometimes, I wish I could close my eyes and when I open them, I'd be somewhere else, like a deserted island where there is no need to fit in or find popularity. The animals won't care how tall I am, and if I'm starving, it won't matter what brand of jeans I wear.

The final bell rings, and Mrs. Maraschino begins her lecture on the nature of our experiment. Our search to find out why her chemistry didn't mesh with her fiancé's. A love potion, perhaps.

If you ask me, I think love is yet another four-letter word.

▫▫ TWIN ▫▫

The girl in the mirror looks like me but isn't me. I don't wear bubblegum pink lipstick or glitter clips in my hair sprayed hair. I don't wear high heels or short dresses like the one my twin reflection pulls down. I wouldn't be caught dead out in public like...

"Shai," I say aloud.

I throw off her heels, bend over, and shake out my hair. Jet black strands swing free, and I tuck them behind my ears. Her dress hits the floor, soap hits my face, and in a few minutes, I'm in my tank top and torn jeans. "Much better."

With most of the house in darkness, I tiptoe from my bedroom to the kitchen. An end table lamp casts light across Mrs. Cardillo asleep on the couch while reality TV buzzes in the background. Her empty wine glass and snores announce she's down for the night. I slip out the slider onto my back patio, where warm air greets me. I'm tempted to jump in the pool, but my promise to meet Shai wins out in the end as I leave the screen porch, shuffle across crabgrass, and open the side gate where Shai waits.

"I knew you'd come," she says with a smile.

"Of course. Otherwise, you'd have pounded on my window till I showed."

She looks at my clothes and frowns. "What happened to the cute outfit I gave you?"

"I looked too much like you," I say matching her glowing grin.

She fakes hurt. "What's wrong with that?"

We giggle until I notice the green car pulled up to a stop in front of my house occupied by two much older guys I've never seen before. Shai grabs my hand, but I yank free.

"Mal, I know what you're gonna say."

"Who are those guys and why are they parked on my lawn?"

"Jake and Walker. They're juniors and they're giving us a ride to the party."

Tension knots my stomach. "I don't know, Shai. My dad would kill me if he knew I was in a car with boys I don't know."

"First of all, your dad will never find out. Secondly, *I* know them."

"That won't be a winning argument."

"C'mon, Mal. Stop being such a Debbie Downer and trust me." All the times I've trusted Shai and regretted it scroll across my mind. She doesn't seem to remember those times as she skips down my drive and calls over her shoulder, "Dibs on the driver!"

I watch her jump into the backseat then wave me on with her "trust me" grin as the passenger window rolls down. It's only now that I can see the driver and passenger are twins. For some reason, I relax because they're brothers. It's gotta be less likely for them to be homicidal maniacs, right?

"You coming, beautiful?" the passenger asks.

Pins and needles jab at my toes. Sometimes, I wish I wasn't afraid of everything. Tonight, I'm gonna live carefree like Shai.

We park at the end of a long street lined with cars. I'm suddenly uncomfortable again as we step out and begin to stroll arm in arm. The guys pace a few steps ahead.

"I am so happy for Lucas," Shai says. "He's been recruited for varsity football this year, in the ninth grade. He's so going to be scouted by a state college, and I'm not leaving without a date."

"What? Why would you care about that? It's four years from now."

Shai jumps, as if I pinched her. "Why would I—?" She shakes her head. "When he graduates and eventually gets drafted into the NFL, they are going to make a big deal of his humble beginnings. And when they go through his high school pictures on national television, there's gonna be a girlfriend in them, who cheers for him from the sidelines and hugs him when he wins state. *That's* why I care."

I have to stop. "Let me get this straight. You're after this guy so you can be the memory in his future?"

The corners of Shai's mouth turn up. "When you put it that way, it sounds stalky."

"It's not stalky. It's a well-thought-out plan… if he gets drafted."

"Believe me," Shai says, "Lucas is the total package.

I'm happy to waste time on him." We both laugh.

"You girls coming?" One of the twins calls.

"Speaking of packages." Shai skips over to the

17

driver and I'm left with the brother.

Shai's great *most* of the time, but I hate it when she drags me into her games and then I'm stuck somewhere I don't wanna be, expected to fit in. The smart, funny, crazy girl who still watches *Teen Titans, Go!* and kicks butt at trivia and eats macaroni and cheese with a shrimp fork...that's the Shai I love. The one who is always there for me, truly understands me, knows me inside and out, and still wants to be in my life. Everyone else? They get whatever Shai thinks they want her to be.

"What's your name?" Twin Two asks.
"Mahlorie. You?"
"Walker."
"Last name, first name, huh?"
"What?"
"You have a last name as a first name. It's... a popular trend."
"Thanks."
"You're welcome?"
"Don't mention it."

We near the house, which seems to drift farther away with each silent step.

"Are you a cheerleader like Shai?" Walker asks. "Me? No way," I laugh. "I'm more book smart than I am the cheer type."

"Cheer type?"

"Yeah, you know...big smile, big butt. Into parties and popularity and shallow stuff like that." I push loose hair behind my ear as we reach the long driveway. "You play football?"

"No. I'm a shallow cheerleader. Couldn't you tell by my big butt and smile?"

I think all the sound in the world has been sucked away, because I can only hear a dull ring.

"Oh…Sorry."

"Don't mention it," he says.

In a heartbeat, I'm alone on the driveway. Thunder rumbles soft in the distance, but I know better as a Floridian. A storm is coming.

▫▫ SPARKS ▫▫

Noise blasts me as I cross the threshold of the massive two-story mansion into a packed foyer. People spill into the living and dining rooms on either side, then disappear into the kitchen beyond. I scan the faces for Shai, faces I barely recognize. Music blares from the speakers, bounces off marble floors, and hits twenty-foot ceilings.

Shai waves me over from the kitchen. "Wanna drink?" She hands me a red Solo cup.

The driver holds a drink in his hand. Looks like I may have to find another way home. "No thanks," I tell Shai.

"Whatever you want." She keeps both cups and throws herself at her twin, who seems to enjoy the attention.

There's a commotion behind me, and I turn right as two guys in a headlock barrel in my direction. Someone yanks me out of the way before they crash into the coffee table and tumble to the floor. Lucas and his best friend, Keegan, jump in to break up the fight with the help of a couple other guys.

"You okay?" Walker asks.

"Yeah. Thanks."

He polishes off his drink and goes for a refill. "Twin Taxi" is not in my future. I'll have to Uber my way home, and hope they take IOUs, because I'm broke. Lucas screams at the two guys who both blame each other while Keegan shows them to the door with both fists.

"Wanna get some fresh air?" Walker asks.

I allow him to take my hand and lead me through the crowd to the back patio that backs up to the Florida swamp. The noise dies down, and the cool air refreshes. Shai and Twin One grab some lounge chairs and we all sit.

"The cops are totally gonna bust this up," Shai says. "Whose house is this? Where are their parents?" I imagine they are unaware of the throw-down on their coffee table.

"Who cares," Twin One says. "What are you, an informer?"

"Leave her alone, Jake," Shai says. "Come on, Mal. Let's go check in on the guest of honor." She locks arms with me, gives her signature pout to Jake for his bad behavior, and removes herself as his punishment. I love that about her, how confident she is with her effect on people. Her power of persuasion. But as we enter the noisy house, I'm reminded that it's also the reason I hate her right now.

Lucas stands near the entertainment center, where Shai drags me over. "Hey, Lucas. Cool party," she says. "Oh, hey, Shai. Glad you could make it." He nods at me. "What's up, Mal?"

"Never been better."

He smirks. "So, what are you girls up to?"

"Oh, nothing." She scoots closer. "We wanted

21

to see how you were after that fight."

"Aren't you the sweetest."

Shai grins. "So, what's up with varsity? You made the team, right?"

Lucas shrugs. "Coach didn't want any spoilers. He makes the announcement on Monday."

Shai bounces into cheerleader mode, her squeals and claps outside the laws of sound. "That's freaking awesome, Lucas! Oh, my God. You must be so excited."

"It's pretty cool."

"Congratulations," I add. "Next stop, you'll be sharing your humble beginnings after the NFL draft."

Shai glares at me while Lucas goes into an uncomfortable pantomime of fingers through hair.

I try not to laugh as Shai adds, "What Mal means is this is a great first step for whatever your future brings."

"Want me to take a picture—?" I ask, but I'm interrupted when Shai nudges me. She mouths, "You're not funny," but her smirk betrays her. Satisfied, I face Lucas and ask, "Is there another bathroom besides the one downstairs?" I don't have to go, but I do need a place to hide while I wait for Shai.

"Upstairs, down the hall, to the left."

"I'll catch up with you later," Shai says, then mouths, "Thank you."

I swim through the sea of faces that part as I climb the stairs two at a time. The dark hall somehow mutes the party below in an otherworldly sort of way. I walk alone through a normal house where pictures line the walls: island vacations, holidays, and family birthdays, followed by sepia-tinted faces and black-and-whites with cracked edges.

I trace my fingers across them. *Who are they?*

What's their story? I open the first closed door. A guest bedroom with a beach theme. Seashell lamps and conch shell decorations with Key West colored walls and throw rug. Across the hall in the next room, the scent of leather-bound books carries from the extensive home office library. I creep inside and close the door behind me. The books are mostly resource types. Encyclopedias set with gold letters on the spines, tons of law books, and books on every historical event you could imagine. A real history buff, but I guess if you love law, you have a soft spot for history.

History repeats itself.

Footfalls hurry off the stairs and down the hall peppered with a girl's giggles. I pray whoever they are, they don't come in this room, but as the door opens I lunge behind the small chaise beneath the window.

"It's a library," a girl says. "Let's go somewhere else."

Yes, let's.

"Wait, wait, wait," a guy answers. "It could be kinda quiet."

Oh, God, no!

Giggle. "I don't know, Zak." Shuffle. "Come on, Audrey." More giggles.

More shuffles. Door opens, then closes. Silence.

After a few moments pass, I lounge on the chaise, glad I'm alone again, and stare out the window. Thunder rumbles and a night sky masks the storm from sight. Fat raindrops patter on the skylight. Lightning flashes to illuminate the angry clouds. Great. The whole party will move inside. Not in here, I hope. I lie back and close my eyes as my own storm rages inside. Why do I let Shai drag me into her scene? It's fine when we're here together, but what am I supposed to do while she tries to hook up with Lucas? Next time she asks, I will tell her no. A firm no. No matter how fun she promises it will be because this isn't fun for me. I don't drink. I don't do parties.

Suddenly I have the feeling that I'm not alone anymore. My eyes shoot open, heart in overdrive. Walker is in creeper mode, just staring at me. "Can I help you with something?" I ask through as much sarcasm as I can muster.

He sits on the chaise beside me and I bolt up. Now I'm the one staring at him. "What's the matter with you?"

"Relax, Mahlorie. You know, you're real pretty when you sleep."

"Says no one to a stranger…..ew!"

"Don't be like that. I was just having a little fun."

Before I can reply, he kisses me. Just like that! No warning, no asking, obviously no idea how to tell when a girl likes him or not.

I push him off, wipe my mouth with the back of my hand.

"What's your problem?" he asks, standing up and putting space between us.

"You are, Walker. You're my problem."

Shaking his head as he moves toward the door, he says, "Shai said you were cool."

"Well, I'm sorry to disappoint you."

He flashes a smile. "Maybe we got off on the wrong foot."

"One of us did," I answer. "I'm trying to apologize."

"Not interested."

He gives me a nasty glare and leaves the room, slamming the door closed behind him. I fall back onto the chaise and stare at the ceiling.

"What a complete jerk."

After several minutes fuming by myself, I decide to leave. I don't even say a word as I hop downstairs and barrel through the crowd to the front door. I don't bother to look for Shai, who obviously gave that guy some false pretensions about me. With no way home and no idea what to do next, I walk out of the neighborhood to the highway.

The calm thunder from earlier has brought hurricane force gales and sideways rain that slices my skin. "You've got to be kidding me!" I am so mad at Shai for making me come to this stupid party. Through tears, I race into the storm and down the street. Lightning flashes, the world a bluish hue that seems unnatural. The hands of God clap in approval.

I veer off the side street onto the two-lane highway framed with palms and spruce trees that moan in the wind. I think there's a 7-11 about a mile up the road, which is where I'm headed. Unless I can catch a ride from a stranger, which I know is a terrible idea, but it's better than a lightning strike, isn't it? No sooner than I think it, a bolt slashes into the earth too close for comfort. I rush faster, pump my legs harder, in search of anyone dumb enough to drive in this storm and pick up a soaked girl afraid of her own shadow. At the moment, the road is clear. *Who'd drive in this weather?* Branches dump leaves. Wind snatches loose bark. Did that jerk really think I wanted him to make his move on me? Like some silly character in one of my mom's stupid smut books?

I scream as lightning splits the air, so close the static raises my hair, thunder so instantaneous it's hard to separate the two. The sky lights up in a brilliant white that bleaches the world around me. I gasp, breathless, as my body goes limp and I roll into the retention ditch and out of sight from the main road. I can't move my muscles.

Am I dead?

Unable to catch my breath, water pricks my skin and puddles around me. My heart thunders in my ears. The storm continues its relentless assault as my senses shut down and I begin to lose consciousness.

▫▫ VOICES ▫▫

My mother's voice awakens me, which is odd. Isn't she at a conference in Miami? I open my eyes to light that slices my skull. "She's awake," Mom says.

I try to sit but feel heavy.

"Don't move, turtledove." Dad sits at the foot of my bed.

"Dad? What are you…?" My voice disappears like a card in a good trick.

"Shhh. Don't talk either."

Great. Dad too? He was in the middle of the Atlantic. Did I die? Was I brought back to life? No, that's stupid. But what if I slipped into a coma and have been here for months…or years? Was Dad's hair always that gray? Does Mom's face look wrinkled?

"What…day?"

Mom hushes me. "It's Tuesday, lambkin. You've been asleep for a few days."

Lambkin. Mom's term of endearment for me based off her favorite author, Shakespeare, from some historical play about King Henry. Wait, did she say Tuesday? "What happened?" I croak.

"Well, turtledove, seems you were struck by lightning. Or near close." Dad's fake smile fades.

"What possessed you to run through the woods in a thunderstorm?"

The storm. The party. It comes back in painful waves.

"Bob, please," Mom interjects. "Not now."

"When then? Next time, when it's too late? When Mal disappears?" Dad waves his magician's jazz hands when he says the word. Probably doesn't even realize it.

"Of course, not," Mom says. "I mean really, Bob, don't you think your melodrama is better suited for the stage? Yes, Mahlorie made some dumb choices..." She stares at me. "...but after this scene's over, she'll make better decisions and follow a whole new path."

There goes Victoria M. Reddish, writing my life as if she plots my character arc in her next bestseller. Sometimes I think Mom cares more about the characters in her books than about me. Mom and Dad continue to argue on my behalf. "Ridiculous," I mumble under my breath.

"It *is* ridiculous," the voice in my head whispers.

Great, now I'm talking to myself. Probably a side effect from the rush of one-billion volts through my body. I can't believe I'm alive. I wonder how long I'll be stuck here.

Mom and Dad finally agree to disagree. They get along much better when there's a lot of land between them. It's ironic because both of my parents make their living by an illusion that they sell to the public while in private, they're totally different people. Dad, with a sleight of hand, can make you see only what he wants you to see.

"It's all about presentation, turtledove, how

you look and where you look. Get the crowd to believe what you want them to believe. See? The magic is how well you sell it. Your pitch. Your package. In this world, people will believe the truth is whatever you show them it is. Appearance is everything."

Mom, on the other hand, creates these perfect worlds in opposition of the one in which she lives, tied up neatly in the end through the power of love. Her appearance is her ticket. How she looks affects how fans perceive her. Once, Mom actually paid a team of marketers to determine which color pant suit she should wear. By her outfit change, she sold 5,000 books and landed a guest spot on *The Today Show*.

"Appearance is everything, lambkin. You won't be

successful as a woman without purposed wardrobe, hair, and make-up. People don't really care about who you are until they see that you fit the mold. Understand? You can be whoever you want to be so long as you make it believable."

This, by the way, is the only reason I got these stupid braces. It's also the reason why I hate short dresses and glittery barrettes. It isn't that I don't want to be popular like Shai. What if I can't? What if no matter how well I sleight my hand or how often I change my clothes, I never find my place? That failure scares me more than not fitting in. So, what do I do? I manipulate my personality, tweak my appearance, and blend.

Where does that leave me?

Somewhere in my dad's deck of cards or my mom's perfectly constructed novel where I blend into a false reality and play the role I'm supposed to play. "Appearance is everything."

"Appearance is nothing," the voice in my head

contradicts, only this time, I'm not certain the voice is mine.

▫▫ STRUCK ▫▫

The odds of a lightning strike are 1 in 960,000. Lucky me.

My experience was called a side flash or a lightning arc off a nearby object—in my case a tree—that sent volts through the air into the closest object. Again, me. It could've been way worse. As a native Floridian, I'm schooled in the power of the lightning bolt. I know to avoid open fields, open water, and open umbrellas when outdoors in a summer storm. Apparently, the trees had acted as conduits, and I was the lightning's final resting place.

Besides my overactive snooze fest, I appear normal. All my tests came back negative and the doctors can't find even a singed arm hair. If it weren't for the place they found me and the nearby charred tree, no one would have even known I was hit by lightning. Early Saturday morning, some guy drove down the highway and caught sight of a teenager near the shoulder. They stopped to help me but found I was barely breathing. The ambulance showed up, my parents were called, and days later I woke up in the hospital. Discharged and home, I'm now expected to recover, which makes no sense to me. I can't even use my cell phone, as a precaution due to static electricity. *There's nothing wrong with me, people!*

I'm stuck at home with my parents who are suddenly on patrol 24-7 to check in on me like I'm a wounded animal they might have to put down. It's like a prison sentence. I kind of wish I could force myself back into that unconscious stage and get away, but that's not an option. And I don't really mean it. The truth is I like both of my parents home to fuss over me for a change instead of stupid arguments about stuff that doesn't matter.

Mom taps on the door and walks into my bedroom. She sets a tray topped with a bowl of tomato soup and a grilled cheese sandwich on my bed. I don't think she's made me this since I was four years old. "Hi, lambkin. How do you feel?"

"Fine, like I was five minutes ago when you asked. You don't need to treat me like I'm an invalid."

She looks hurt. "I am your mother, and it is my job to make sure that you are well taken care of. Your survival of a near-death experience is a miracle, Mahlorie. You do understand the odds of survival after a lightning strike are astronomical." I stare into my soup to avoid eye contact with my mom. "I would love for you to tell me what it felt like when the lightning flashed off the tree."

I look up in disbelief, a large bite of grilled cheese stuffed in my mouth. "Oh, my God, Mom. Are you studying me for character development?"

Mom smooths out her pants to avoid my gaze. "Not particularly, I mean I don't have a character in mind, if that's what you're asking. But it's good to take notes."

I shovel in more sandwich. "I can't believe you."

"Now, Mahlorie, you don't have to be like that."

"Like what, Mom? Upset that you're exploiting my experience to sell more books?"

"Books reflect life, lambkin. What you've been through is a miracle, and it could impact a reader who has been through a similar tragedy. You owe it to that person to share your story."

"You can leave now."

I love my mother, but I *hate* Victoria M. Reddish.

"Well, it's apparent that you are out of sorts today." Mom stands and heads to the door. She faces me before she goes and says, "I'll come back later for your tray."

Somehow, I feel guilty for what I've said, and now my appetite is gone.

As I set the half-eaten tray of food on the dresser, pain slices through my skull. My palms press into my temples to match the pressure without any luck. It's like a bomb went off inside my head. I fall to the floor, the pain now paired with a shrill shriek that threatens to knock me back into unconsciousness. I don't know how much more of this I can take. My teeth grind together and tears form in my eyes. I worry my head is about to crack in half like an egg, when it all…stops.

It takes me a moment to lower my hands after the pain dulls to a thud and the shriek silences. "What happened?" I say out loud.

Could it be a delayed concussion? No way I would tell Mom what happened. You think she's on my back now? She'd camp out in my room for sure and stare at me like a lab rat in a cage—and probably take notes for her next novel.

There's a knock on my door, then it opens. Dad stands in the doorway. "I heard you scream. Are you okay?"

"Fine," I lie. "Just a little headache."

"A little? That didn't sound like a little."

"Dad, I'm fine." I stand to get back in bed. "It's gone now. It was no big deal...really." Dad would freak out if I told him that I'd felt Thor's hammer slam into my skull as if it were a nail head. You don't say stuff like that to your parents, you know?

As he steps into my bedroom, Dad says, "Listen, honey, I know you're probably not ready for a lecture, but—"

"Dad, do we have to do this now?"

"Yes, Mahlorie. I'm sorry, but I don't understand why you were in the middle of the woods in the middle of a thunderstorm. Furthermore, I don't understand why you were at a house party with no parents there, when you were supposed to be home under the supervision of Mrs. Cardillo."

"The supervision of a wino?"

Dad doesn't speak, which is worse than if he had exploded. I let out a deep breath. "It was stupid, okay? I shouldn't have done it and it'll never happen again."

Dad sits at the foot of the bed. It's like he and Mom read the same parenting manual. "Listen, turtledove, you'll always be my little girl, but you're only my responsibility for four more years. I can only hope to give you all the tools you'll need..." Dad waves his hands and I know he's about to do a magic trick. "...to succeed." Somehow, he makes my cell phone appear in his hands. "Doctor said you could use it now."

I take my connection to the world with a smile. "Thanks, Dad."

"Shai called. She wanted to know if she could come by and see you."

"All right. I'll call her back."

Dad kisses my head, then crosses to the door. He faces me and asks, "Should I be worried about you?"

In truth, I say, "No, Dad. Not at all." And for a split second I actually believe myself.

▫▫ TWEAKED ▫▫

Shai shows up a few hours later with a basket of popcorn, some candy, and her mom's VHS of *Back to the Future,* which irks me to no end because, first of all, I don't own a VHS player, which Shai knows, and second off, I don't appreciate the attempt at humor on her part—though truthfully, it's pretty hilarious—to watch a movie focused around a lightning bolt that changed the main character's entire life.

The candy, I take without question.

In Shai's defense, she hooks up an old VHS player she brought with her. It's one of my favorites to do with Shai, chill in front of the television and talk. But I don't feel it today. And not because I almost died, either. I'm just off, you know? Mom has "postponed her schedule" for future bookings but still leaves town in three days for a romance writer's convention in Denver, where she's the Keynote.

"Can't get out of this one, lambkin."

Yeah, I know. Appearance is everything.

Dad leaves tomorrow for a seven-day cruise on the Mediterranean. It's a pirate-themed gig and was Dad's idea. Half the rooms were booked in advance by fans and fellow magicians, who saw this as an opportunity to rub elbows with Dad.

"Can't get out of this one, turtledove."

Of course, you can't.

If I'd actually been fried by that bolt of lightning, would Mom and Dad have missed the funeral and sent flowers with their condolences? "Do they even care?" I whisper.

"Yes, they do," I hear in reply.

I jump up, the hairs on the back of my neck on end. Shai stares at me. "Are you okay, Mal?"

I look around for a ghost or Jiminy Cricket, find neither, and shovel a handful of popcorn in my mouth. "Yeah. Sorry…brain's tweaked."

"What's new?" She smirks. "Not funny."

We watch the film. Shai says, "Michael J. Fox was such a hottie. I wonder if time travel were possible, do you think if people left letters for their earlier selves with advice, would they listen like Doc did? You know, recommend they buy stock in Apple early in the game. Or plead that they don't get that horrid hairstyle in the sixth grade?"

"That was not my fault," I say, mouth agape. "It was an 80s phase… how was I supposed to know that she would give me an old lady perm instead of a body wave?"

Shai grins from ear to ear. "Why would you ever get a perm to begin with?"

"Did you not hear me? 80s phase."

Shai throws a piece of popcorn at me. It bounces off my cheek, and we laugh. We're back to the film, when Shai says, "I love your hair. I think you have the prettiest hair I've ever seen."

"Whatever, Barbie hair."

"Ha!" Shai spits out popcorn and we both fall

into rifts of laughter.

"Why's Barbie hair funny?" I hear a voice clearly ask.

I fall off the bed, and Shai jumps up to help me.

It's exactly like that scene, when Marty tries to get away from his teenage mother, but in my case, it's a phantom voice I'm afraid no one else can hear but me. "Did you hear that?" I ask, fearful of Shai's answer.

"Hear what?"'

"Shai, tell me you just asked why Barbie hair is so funny."

"Why would I ask you that? I'm the one who said it."

"Then who—?"

"Wait. Can you hear me?"

I pace the room, hands a pool of sweat as nausea churns my stomach.

"Mal, what's wrong with you? Are you all right?"

"Hello? You still there?"

I cover my ears, hum to cover the voice, and scan my room for the radio left on or the polite serial killer with good conversation skills as Shai says, "You've been acting weird since I got here."

"Seriously, Shai? I was struck by lightning and almost died. All because I was at some stupid party that you insisted I go to where some dumb guy thought I was actually interested in him enough to kiss me without asking."

"That sounds serious," the voice in my head says.

"It *is* serious."

"You can *hear me,"* the voice says. "Lighten up, Mal. I never said it wasn't."

I press my hands to my ears again. "Stop

talking!"

"What is your problem?"

My hands drop. "I'm not talking to you, Shai."

"Then who are you talking to?"

"Dyson. Say my name out loud."

"No, no, no! I won't," I say. "Won't what?" Shai asks. *"Dyson. Say it!"*

"I'm gonna get your mom," Shai says.

"D-Y-S-O-N...Dyson!"

"Shut up!" I scream my ears uselessly covered by my hands.

"Excuse me?"

"Not. You. Shai."

"Mal, you're freaking me out."

"Say it, and I swear I'll shut up," I hear in my head. Helplessly, I whisper, "Dyson," and the voice stills. Shai stares at me like I belong in an insane asylum, but the voice in my head is gone. I cry. Shai drops beside me on the bed.

"What's the matter with me?" I ask.

"Nothing. There's nothing the matter with you. You've been through a serious trauma. That doesn't go away easy, you know? Soldiers aren't the only ones who go through PTSD." She brushes my hair from my eyes and hands me a box of tissues. "Why don't you get some sleep? Okay? You can call me later if you feel like talking."

I nod and fall back on my pillow. Shai turns off the television and closes the door behind her. Under her breath, she mumbles how she'd mention to my mom I wanted my room vacuumed. My eyes shut, but a thought nags me away from sleep: *Can lightning lead to schizophrenia?*

⌑⌑ NOT ALONE ⌑⌑

Monday I'm back to school despite my petitions. I throw on a gray pullover with dark jeans to blend into the drab walls of my school.

No such luck.

If the evidence of my lightning strike had only been my unruly hair that has developed a slight spiral curl from the jolt—like the one I had wanted in the sixth grade, by the way—I might have been able to play it off. However, it seems the event went viral.

"What did it feel like?"

"Did it hurt?"

"Did your life flash before your eyes?"

"Do you have a Harry Potter mark?" *God, what is wrong with everyone?*

Questions assault me from every angle. I can't even hear myself think, which is kind of good because I'm worried that voice might find its way to my ears again. Someone slips a piece of paper in my hand that reads "call me" with a random phone number, another one smells my singed hair.

Get me out of here!

"Back off, simpletons and leave Mal alone."

Lucas Chambers, with his voice alone, scatters

the cockroaches. He wraps his arm across my shoulders and leads me to a study room I didn't even know existed. Shai waits inside. Tears sting my eyes and she holds me in a motherly embrace.

"I gotcha," she whispers. "You're okay."

"How'd you know?" I ask.

"Lucas and I were in here studying when we heard the commotion. I knew it was about you. I just knew."

"Studying, huh?" I pull free, wipe my cheeks dry. She shrugs with a warm smile.

"You need a bodyguard," Lucas decides. "I'll grab Aaron McPherson. He's the biggest defensive lineman we've got. Dumb as rocks, but enough brawn to keep anyone even half as smart from messing with you."

"I'll be okay."

"You wanna think about it?"

The image of the paparazzi in the hall chokes me with claustrophobia. "Well, maybe to first period."

"You got it. Be right back."

Lucas leaves, and Shai squeezes my arm. "Isn't he amazing?"

"Actually, yeah. He's a lot nicer than I thought."

"I told you. Perfect package."

I shake my head. "You're so weird."

"Whatever, Miss Popularity. I'm so jealous. I've never been the center of attention for the entire student body."

"Get struck by lightning."

She pauses, as if in consideration. "Maybe I will." Part of me believes her.

Lucas returns with Aaron, a six-foot-plus

sophomore who pushes two-hundred pounds and sports a buzz cut, with biceps wider than my thighs.

"Woah," I utter, involuntarily.

"Aaron, this is Mahlorie Moore," Lucas says. "You are to guard her with your life today, got it? No one gets near her. No one."

"No prob," Aaron says. A Boston accent stains his words.

"It's really not necessary all day," I mumble. "Just to first period."

"No prob," he replies.

I see now that Lucas's description of him was not far from the truth.

□ □ □ □ □

A defensive lineman leads me down the hall and it's the safest I've felt since the womb. Students literally shuffle out of his way without a word, which is good because I think all he knows is "no prob."

We reach first period Algebra class and he pauses at the door to let me through. "I'm good from here," I tell him. "You don't need to walk me around all day. But thanks. I really appreciate it."

"You're welcome," he says with a wink and a gun finger before he barrels away.

I slide low in my seat to hide from Ms. Lichtim's line of sight with Tristan Jones's head as a barrier. It works for half the period, but when she scribbles one of her infamous problems on the board, my energy color must glow fluorescent, because she calls me out. With a groan, I stomp up and grab a blue marker, then read the math hieroglyphs I'm supposed to decipher. "Okay," I say under my breath. "$(7x-2)^{(1/3)} + (7x+5)^{(1/3)} = 3$. Welp. At least I can read it." That makes me smile.

"Something funny, Miss Moore?"

"Oh, no, Ms. Lichtim. There's nothing funny at all about Algebra."

That warrants me some laughter from around the room and a stern look from my teacher. I quickly face the board, my cheeks flush with heat. I want to sit down, and we all know these problems are Math Superstar level, a place I will never visit. I say, "Forty- two," as I write it on the whiteboard, since everybody knows forty-two is the answer to the meaning of life, when an almost audible voice whispers, *"The answer is 3/7."*

Tingles flood me as I side-glance to see who said that. The only person close enough is Ms. Lichtim, and she'd never give an answer away. My palms sweat. The marker hovers over my answer when I hear, *"I'm telling you, it's 3/7. Why are you gonna get it wrong on purpose?"*

The marker falls to the floor and I bend over and catch my breath. "Shut up," I whisper to...to who? To no one. It's all my imagination. There's no voice in my head, especially not a boy's.

"You gonna pretend you can't hear me or write the correct answer?"

I get to my feet, change my solution, and rush to my desk.

Ms. Lichtim looks the problem over and says in disbelief, "That is correct, Miss Moore."

All eyes turn on me, the girl who can't do math to save her life. It seems they won't stop without an explanation. I can't say a voice in my head told me to do it. I could swear I'd watched a lot of *Good Will Hunting* over the weekend. Finally, I say, "I got hit by lightning. Must have short-circuited the wiring."

Somehow, it's enough, and Ms. Lichtim continues with the lesson.

I've got to get out of here. My hand shoots up as I ask, "Ms. Lichtim, may I use the restroom?"

"Of course," she says, with a smile.

I've never known this woman to smile at any student. Without question, I snatch the hall pass from her desk and head to the closest restroom. Before I lock myself in a stall, I check to see if I'm alone. I breathe for several long minutes before I get the courage to say, "Dyson, can you hear me?"

There's an even longer pause before the boy in my head answers, *"Yes."*

▫▫ FIGURATIVELY ▫▫

It's as if the world stops. "How is this possible?" I ask.

"I have no idea," Dyson says. *"This is incredible!"*

Not quite the words I would use. "How'd you get in my head?"

"I started to hear you, well someone, faintly, like a voice under water, you know? Crazy. Your voice grew louder till I could make out words and...this is...I can't believe you can hear me."

"None of this seems weird to you?"

"Of course, it's weird," he says. *"It's the strangest, most incredibly bizarre occurrence that's ever happened to me."*

"That makes two of us."

The bathroom door opens, and I shush Dyson, who doesn't get it. He babbles in my ear as the door opens and the stall next to me is occupied.

"You there?" I hear. *"Hello? Where'd you go?"*

"Not alone," I whisper.

The girl in the stall next to me asks, "Are you talking to me?"

"Nope."

"Okay." She drags out the word.

"You talking to me now?" Dyson asks. *"You alone again? What's your name anyway?"*

"Shut up," I seethe.

"What's your problem?" the girl says with a bite. "Not. You," I shout.

I see her brown hair brush the floor as she bends forward to see me. I push my backpack to block her view. "Mahlorie? Is that you?"

Oh, my God. She knows me. "Nope," I lie. "You got me confused. My name's…" I look around, desperate for some help. My gaze rests on the toilet paper dispenser. "Jamar…"

"Seriously?" Dyson says. *"As in Sam Jamar, like the bathroom supply company?"*

Of course, he would know that useless tidbit of information.

"Stop. Talking," I shout.

"I didn't say anything," Nosey says, as she flushes and leaves the stall.

"Not talking to you. God!"

"You tell her, Jamar,*"* Dyson ribs, hysterical with laughter.

"I swear to God if I could, I would hit you right now."

"You need help," Nosey says, while she leaves the bathroom. "Freak."

"Not you!" I call after her. Dyson still cackles in my head. "Great. She thinks I just threatened, her thanks to you."

"No, she doesn't. She thinks Jamar threatened her." And Dyson starts into another wave of laughter.

"Is there an off switch? Don't you have some

work you should be focused on?" The bell rings as his laughter quiets. "Listen, Dyson. I've gotta get to class, and I can't do it with you in my head. I don't know why we can hear each other, but I need it to stop so I can think, okay?"

"No, I get it. This is weird for me, too. I tend to joke a lot when I'm nervous. How about this: I'll stay out of your head unless you say my name."

"You can do that? Keep a distance, I mean."

"It's hard to explain, but I have to focus to make out what you say, like a radio frequency that barely comes in and then suddenly reads loud and clear. Otherwise, it's white noise."

The hall fills with students, and I know the bathroom won't be quiet for long. "Give me till the end of the day, all right?"

"Sure."

I stand, already lighter with the knowledge I'll be alone till seventh period. But chills creep across my skin that Dyson could be lying.

"What's your real name?"

Should I tell him? Do I trust him? What if he's a mass murderer? How do I even know his real name's Dyson? I mean, who names their kid after a vacuum cleaner? "For now, call me Jamar," I say.

"Right," he says coldly. And then, he's gone.

◻◻ TUNE IN ◻◻

My day runs smoothly without any interruptions from the boy in my head. I'm a train wreck, of course, unable to focus, and the new Mahlorie Moore Fan Club follows me around like I'm a reality TV star. Why did my parents make me come back to school so soon again? Oh yeah, it interfered with their schedules. Mrs. Cardillo was let go after Friday's incident, so when my parents go back to work I may get to finally stay alone. Doubtful. Near the end of the day, my phone vibrates. It's a text from Mom: *Your cousin, Philip, will stay with you this week. I'm headed to the airport to get him now.* ♥

God, no! Philip? He's not even my real cousin. He's my uncle's wife's nephew, which makes him a relative only by marriage. We share no blood relation. When we were younger, Philip would send me these god-awful letters about how his love for me was deeper than the deepest oceans and how I was more beautiful than the most beautiful summer sunset. He's a total tool, yet for some reason, my parents have always insisted we hang out. I'm barely fifteen, and he turned eighteen last summer, which puts us legally outside the "friends" zone, but my babysitter? I'd rather be stuck with Mrs. Cardillo.

I text Mom back one word:
No.
That's all I have to say about that.

□□□□□□

The longest day of my life finally ends. I walk home alone, to contemplate whether I want to talk with Dyson or not when the powerful engine of a muscle car rumbles closer. I glance over my shoulder as a black Impala creeps to a stop beside me. I don't recognize the driver, and panic constricts my throat. Do I run for it? How far could I make it before that beast mobile ran me down? When did I become so paranoid?

Then Shai's face pops up from the backseat, alongside Lucas's. "Hey, pretty mama, you need a lift?" she catcalls.

My whole body relaxes. "Hey, Shai. Nah, I'm good."

"You sure?"

"Rough day. Call you later?" She pouts. "Okay. Love you."

"Love you too."

The driver hits the gas and the car speeds off, confirmation I'd made the right choice. "Mouth breathers," I murmur.

I turn off the main street onto backroads. I know it'll be a longer walk, but I have a lot on my mind. Tentatively, I make the decision, and say, "Dyson, you there?"

There is no answer for a short while, and I doubt he even exists, which is probably for the best anyway. Confident in this realization, I shuffle soundlessly across the dirt path carved through the woods like a memory that can't be shaken. Wind rustles branches and leaves. Birds exchange secrets. I wonder if animals can hear me too? I concentrate my thoughts on the squirrel that clings to a tree trunk, and whisper, "The force is strong with you, young squirrel."

As I'm about to reach out and touch the creature, I hear, *"What are you, Yoda?"*

I scream, and the squirrel runs off as the tree empties of birds. "Dang it, Dyson! You scared me to death."

He laughs. *"I was trying to rescue that poor squirrel from your Jedi mind trick."*

"You're such a nerd," I say, though the smile in my voice betrays me.

"Okay, squirrel whisperer."

I walk steady. "Still think this is weird?"

"Yup. You?"

"Weirdest ever," I say.

"Can you hear everything or just my voice?"

"Everything?"

"Yeah, like right now I'm playing music. Can you hear it?"

"No."

"Give me a sec."

"Hadn't planned to go anywhere." After a short pause, the faint sound of music trickles in the distance, but I can hear it. "How did you do that?"

"You hear it?"

"Barely. Who is it?"

"It's by A Great Big World, one of my favorites. "Say Something." I have headphones on, but…It's cool that you can hear it too."

Why can I hear any of this? *"So, Dyson, where do you go to school?"*

"I don't."

"I knew it. You are a figment of my imagination."

His voice smiles. *"I'm homeschooled. Always have been."*

"Really? You've never been in a classroom before?"

"I'm homeschooled, not living in ahut."

I reach the edge of the woods backed up to my neighborhood.

"I won't ask where you go to school," he says.
"Why not?"

"Because you'll tell me Arm & Hammer High School or some ridiculous made up name, like Jamar."

"Listen, this is all hard to digest and figure out. It's different for girls. I don't expect you to understand."

Dyson doesn't respond. "Besides, you can hear me way more than I can hear you."

"What's that mean?"

"Well, it feels to me like you can hear every word I say, even when I don't talk directly to you. Like you're always ready to respond the way Alexa is. I'm a pretty private person, Dyson, and with you in my head all the time…You can hear everything, can't you?"

"Yes."

"Then why can't I hear you?" The music stops. Dead quiet.

"BecauseI don't talk unless I know you're listening."

▫▫ REVEAL ▫▫

"There's my favorite cousin!"

While I sit relaxed on the couch in boy shorts and a tank top, Philip's shrill voice breaks glass from across the room. "Somebody shoot me now," I whisper.

"What's wrong?" Dyson pipes in.

"Tell ya later. Shut up till I say your name." Radio silence.

Philip rushes around the corner, arms extended. "Mahlorie," he says. "My favorite cousin in the whole world. Come on and give me a big hug."

I stand, and feel my face take on that look you get when you reach out to an empty toilet paper roll in the middle of the night.

He frowns. "You gonna make me beg for one?"

That's not a bad idea, but Mom's facial expression informs me I have the wrong plan. I lean in for a quick hug and turn my face at the last minute to avoid a kiss on the lips. Somehow, Mom misses that part. Figures. "Well, aren't you grown up?" he says, as he looks me up and down. Mom misses that too. "You still draw?"

"Not so much." I catch Mom's steely gaze. "Still write redundant poetry?"

"I wrote a special poem for you on the plane. Maybe I can read it later."

I cringe.

"You two always got along so well," Mom interjects from the kitchen. "Isn't that nice, Mahlorie, that you inspired his poetry?"

The best way to get on Mom's good side is to write. Now that I think about it, I bet that's why she likes Philip so much. He's a writer at heart, has been since he was little boy, and Mom always coaches him like he's the prodigy I never could be. Here I thought it was for my benefit that he came around.

"Yeah, Mom. Real nice, if you like love letters from your cousin."

"Oh, Mahlorie," Mom replies. "Don't be so self- absorbed."

My eyes literally bug in my head. "*Me* don't be self- absorbed?"

"Well, yes. You think Philip writes about you simply because he shares his poetry with you. It's rare to find a young man so in touch with his emotions."

"I don't think that's what he's in touch with," I mutter.

"Mahlorie, enough," Mom states.

"Actually, Aunt Vickie, she's not too far off about how my poems are for her," Philip says.

"Oh?" Mom replies.

He's got my attention, too.

"Mahlorie is my muse. I know it's kind of sappy, but I always write beautiful words when I think of her."

Bile tickles my throat. Surely Mom isn't naive enough to believe this crap.

"Oh, Philip, that's lovely," my gullible mother replies. "You are an old soul."

Philip beams.

I gag.

Mom drinks the Kool-Aid.

"Wow," I say. "As much as I'd like to stay, I've got a ton of homework, so I'm headed to my room." I take the stairs like the floor's lava.

"Dinner's in one hour," Mom calls up. "I made reservations at The Crusty Bread."

Great. A fancy, five course meal stuck between someone who lies for a living and someone who lies pathologically.

□□□□□□

The Crusty Bread is an old house renovated into a restaurant. Each small room has been converted to its own private dining area decorated uniquely with mismatched furnishings and antiques to make it feel like you're dining in some old relative's home. A white cloth drapes over the table and, true to its name, hot crusty bread sits in a basket beside soft butter in the shape of roses.

We order appetizers and drinks, and I try my best to become invisible, which doesn't work great for me. Mom and Philip gab on and on, mostly about themselves:

"What's your next book about?"

"How is college?"

"You and Bob both travel a lot for work?"

"How is your mother?"

My ears perk up when Philip asks about Shai. It makes my skin crawl to hear her beautiful name fall from his hideous lips. "What about Shai?" I ask.

"You still friends with her?" Philip questions.

"Why wouldn't I be?"

He scratches the back of his neck as if he wants to tell me something, but not sure how to word it. I dare him to open his big, fat trap with my meanest glare.

"She hasn't outgrown her yet," Mom interjects. My glare shifts to Mom, who continues. "Well, honey, you and Shai have such different goals and personalities. You are destined for greatness, Mahlorie, a state university and career in a field that requires a master's or PhD. If Shai goes to college at all, she'll attend a trade school for cosmetology or massage therapy, both of which are necessary for the world to go around but not the types of careers you aspire for if you dream of success. It's sweet you've remained friends this long, but doubtful it'll last through high school." She flips the pages of her menu. "I think I'll have the Chilean sea bass. What about you, Philip?"

My ears burn. What has been up with my mother lately? She is a completely different person. She used to support whatever I said and did. She was always someone I looked to for advice, and that one person besides Shai that I couldn't wait to spend time with. Lately, she's been so busy with her career, it's like I don't even exist anymore. And now she's on Shai's back too? What happened?

"I'm sorry," I say, "but when did it become *rag on Shai and Mahlorie dinner theater?*" She's not even here to defend herself."

Mom's eyes widen.

Philip frowns. "I'm sorry, Mal. It wasn't my intention to upset you or be a jerk."

Nope, that comes naturally, I want to say back.

"Really, Mahlorie, you're entirely too sensitive. We all like Shai very much."

"We like you way more," Philip says as his

hand squeezes my knee beneath the tablecloth.

I bend back his fingers then knock his hand away. My napkin flies along with it. He makes a face that goes unnoticed by Mom as appetizers arrive. A server sets down escargot in melted butter, and I stomp as hard as I can on Philip's toe. He grimaces and Mom smiles. "It's not nearly as bad as you think," she says.

"I dropped my napkin," I say, and hit the floor. With Mom distracted by snails, I debate escape, out the door, through the restaurant, to anywhere but here. I am a prisoner, trapped in someone else's house. Where's my hero to rescue me?

Dyson.

Should I? I barely know him. I don't trust him. Maybe I never will. Yet he's somehow in my head, supernaturally able to talk to and listen to me like the voice of a conscience, although whether he's the angel or the devil on my shoulder only time will tell. There must be a reason. Doesn't there? Is it possible that this happened on purpose or could it be a freak accident? No, a connection wove us together by unseen threads the way technology transmits across invisible fiber optics, only this web feels more like a spider's, and I wonder if I'm its next meal.

"Dyson?" I whisper. It's quiet.

I wonder again if I've invented him or he's a hallucination from the lightning bolt that might have fried my brain. I'm glad he doesn't answer. It was stupid to call him, like he's a genie that answers to my whims. I'm about to stand when I hear, *"Jamar? That you?"*

Relief.

"Who else would it be? You have a call center in your head?"

Laughter.

"Can you stay for a while?" I ask. "I need to get through this dinner."

"*Sure. What's up?*" Concern colors his words. "I'll explain later. Keep me company?"

"*Always.*"

I hop back up, throw myself into my seat, and grin as if my napkin's retrieval had been one of Venus's trials for Psyche. "Sorry about that," I say, and face Philip. "Did you need one?"

Mom's phone vibrates.

Philip's forehead wrinkles. "Need what?"

"A napkin. I figured you must have lost yours, which is why you were tried to take mine from off my lap."

His face flushes crimson.

Mom doesn't hear, phone glued to her ear. Agent.

Finalize trip. Details.

"*Who's Philip?*" Dyson asks.

"Philip is a disgusting relative who needs to learn to keep his hands to himself," I say to Dyson, but in a way that won't make Philip think I'm crazy.

Philip's jaw tenses. "It's not like that, Mal. You know I don't look at you that way. You're my favorite cousin."

He says that, right as Dyson asks, "*Want me to punch him in the mouth for you?*"

That makes me laugh. Philip thinks my joy was addressed at him and relaxes.

Dyson says, "*You have a great laugh.*"

I feel my cheeks warm. I'm glad he can't see me. But Philip can. Crap. More complications. "Who are you?" I ask Dyson.

As Philip goes into a monologue like a poorly

written villain, Dyson says, *"Well, let's see. I'm seventeen, an Aquarius, and I like to read and write poetry. I hate reality TV, love basketball, and my perfect date would be a romantic stroll on the beach as Siegfried and Roy ride tigers in the background and dolphins perform a water ballet."*

I lose it, my laughter so loud Mom ices me before she walks away for privacy. Philip looks confused as he was in mid-sentence, but quickly laughs along with me as only a shallow jerk could.

Dinner arrives. I take a bite of chicken pesto. "Share some of your poetry with me."

Philip's grin stretches. "Sure," he says. "I'll read what I wrote for you on the plane."

Mom smiles, as Philip reaches in his back pocket to grab the folded sheet of paper. Neither of them knows I am not really at dinner with them.

Dyson says, *"I don't usually share what I've written, but since I wrote this after you popped in my head, I guess it's only fair to read it to you."*

I chew, wait. "Well? Are you gonna read it?" Philip starts right away. I tune him out with ease. I close my eyes.

A deep breath fills my head. *"Twisted maze turns. Your voice my beacon. Walls birth walls. Dead ends stretch to corners with no beginning. Each time I think I've reached you, your hem is all I find, hugs the next branch as you race out of sight. This labyrinth is my prison, not because I can't find the end, but because I know when I do, you'll be gone."*

Tears pool in my eyes. Speechless.

Heart swells.

"Well, say something," Dyson says.

"I don't know what to say." I wipe my eyes, catch Philip's expectant stare. I choose to pretend he doesn't exist, although he still thinks we are engaged in conversation.

"Did you like it?" Dyson asks. "It's beautiful."

I hear a smile in his breath. For the first time, I'm curious what he looks like, what color his eyes are, what his lips are like…

"Glad you like it."

"More. Read more."

"I don't know. The rest aren't nearly as good."

"How modest of you."

That one gets a strange glance from Philip, who says, "I don't have any more with me."

"What makes that one so special?" I ask.

Pause. A beat. Silence. *"Because I wrote it about you."*

Heat spreads out from my stomach. Is this guy for real? He doesn't even know me. I mean, we're in each other's head, which means…what? What does it mean? For all he knows, I'm pimple-faced, short, fat, hideous, every stereotypical appearance that society deems 'ugly'. Then it hits me, no—slaps me in the face. This guy doesn't care. Appearance doesn't matter to him at all. At least not like it does to everyone else I know.

And that scares me to death. I have no idea how to handle someone like him. "I gotta go."

"Did I upset you?" Dyson asks, disappointed.

I dive beneath the table to retrieve my dropped napkin again. "It's not that. If we don't stop now, I'll have to explain later to my mom who the invisible boy was beneath our table at dinner." Mom scoots her chair out. "But, hey, thanks for the company."

"Any time you need me."

I pause. I want to. Should I? Yes! Say it,

Mahlorie. "Dyson?"

"Yes?"

"My name…is Mahlorie."

Quiet.

"Mahlorie," he says. *"That's a real pretty name.*

Way better than Jamar."

"Yeah, I know."

"Catch ya later, Mahlorie."

And then, he's gone.

▫▫ FUN & GAMES ▫▫

At some time in the night, my eyes shoot open. My heart races. Is there someone in my room? I sit up, scan for motion, and click on my end table lamp. The flood of light makes me squint. I'm alone, yet uneasy. What woke me? I check my phone. 3:17 a.m. Too early to get up, and by the time I fall back to sleep, I'll be a zombie when my alarm shrieks in the morning. I roll onto my back, click off the lamp, and stare at the ceiling.

Blink. Breathe. Blink. Clock.

3:21 a.m.

Only four minutes?

I scroll through TikTok, bored. Not one post on Instagram worth my time. I'm not a big believer in social media to begin with, but if you're not in the know, stuff happens. This one girl at a school a few towns over found out that some guy posted they'd been dating…for three months! And she didn't even know him. Could you imagine? Not me. I keep up with social media to be safe. No one's gonna say they hooked up with me and get away with it.

My eyes close, but I still can't sleep. I wonder

about Dyson. Who is he? Where does he live? Is he cute? Why can I hear him? The poem he read scrolls across my mind. So beautiful. So passionate. So dark. Should I be afraid of him? Tell someone? Ignore him? Do I give into curiosity and genuinely get to know him? Why haven't I told Shai yet?

What if he's in my head forever? Now, I definitely can't sleep.

I turn my lamp back on and sit at my desk with pencil and paper. It's been a long while, but I start to draw. A curve. A shadow. A straight line. A face, the one I see in my mind when I hear Dyson's voice, although I will never know if I'm right since I don't plan on us meeting him...ever. But the boy I draw is cute and it makes me want to meet him.

I huff, frustrated.

"You awake?" A whisper.

"Dyson?"

"Do you have plans to meet someone else in your head in the middle of the night?"

"No." I smile.

"Can't sleep?"

"No."

"Me neither. Why'd you huff? That jerk still around?"

"Thank God, no. I'm actually drawing, which is weird."

Dyson's voice lifts. *"Why is it weird?"*

"Because I haven't drawn in a very long time."

"Really? What changed? New inspiration?"

What do I tell him, that my hand is on autopilot because I'm curious to see his face? Sure, Mahlorie, that doesn't scream stalker. It's totally normal. But what about this is normal? Still...

"Mahlorie? You fall asleep?"

Dang, I forgot I told him my name. Flustered, I say, "Sorry, I'm tired and it's late." I quickly throw the paper in the trash and hop back into bed. "Why are you awake?"

"Too much on my mind."

I want to know, but I don't. "Like what?"

"Like why can we talk to each other? How is this even physically possible?" His gravelly voice carries sleep. *"We have to think way off the grid if we really want to know why, like the kind of explanation you'd find in a good 'B' flick on the sci-fi channel."*

"What, like *Sharknado*?"

"Exactly. Weird, fantastic, supernatural even. Because that's what we're dealing with here." Deep breath.

Worry? Nerves? "Maybe," I dare, "we should try to figure out what connects us, what we have in common. It could lead to an answer."

"Not a bad idea. So, tell me all about yourself.

What makes you tick?"

I run my fingers through my hair. "I wish I knew." This is gonna be harder than I thought.

"Well besides art, which you like, and Phil, who you don't, there's not much else I know about you...except that you suck at math."

"Hey, that's not fair. It was a hard question."

"I got it right."

"Well, maybe that's because you're some kind of freaky math genius and not a reflection of my math skills at all."

"You got me."

"Seriously?"

"It's my favorite subject. I love math."

63

"Oh."

"How about you? What's your favorite subject?"

"Summer."

Laughter. *"Not big on academia?"*

"It's not that." I sit up, legs crossed. "They teach us so much stuff that's useless—"

"Like algebra?"

"Yes, like algebra, and they take three times as long as they should to do it. Plus, there's the whole popularity contest and wardrobe and gossip. It's not me."

"That's why I homeschool. I learn what I want, when I want. I'm the most popular kid in my school, and I don't even bother to get dressed some days."

I laugh. "Sounds perfect to me. I'd trade lives in a heartbeat."

"I don't know. From what I've heard so far, I think the short of the end of the stick is falling in my hands, not yours, in that trade."

"Hey!"

"I'm just saying."

His laugh makes me smile. It's quiet between us, and I start to feel sleepy. My fingers click off the lamp and I lay down in the dark. Moonbeams strike the wall.

"You getting tired?" Dyson asks. "A little. You?"

"I could sleep, but I'll hang with you for as long as you want."

I stare at my ceiling. Headlights cross the walls and spread out. Suddenly, I'm tensed. "Dyson, are you scared?"

"Because we can hear each other? No, not at

all. I'm not afraid of much."

"Why not?" Eyelids grow heavy.

There's a pause. *"Things happen every day that are out of our control. Power is an illusion. If the sun doesn't rise tomorrow, what could we do about it? We trust that the seasons will come, that the guy in the lane next to us will stay there, that our locked door will keep bad guys out. But the truth is, we are at the mercy of circumstance. For instance, you're running late and miss your flight. Not a big deal, unless that plane is hijacked by terrorists and flown into the World Trade Center. Why did Death let them off the hook, but not the rest? What choices led them to miss their flight that were out of their control?"*

The air stills, his conviction pure.

"Or you run into an old friend you haven't thought of in years until that very morning when they popped in your head for no apparent reason. Life is a series of moments that are interconnected, some spectacular, others insignificant. But once in a while, the course of your life is changed and after that moment you'll never be the same again. So, no, your voice in my head doesn't scare me at all. It's a moment that's connected us."

I'm speechless. Who is this guy? "I've never met anyone like you before."

"Uh-oh. Is that good or bad?"

"It's good. Most people I know think life is a series of parties. They don't think like you. They don't think like me."

"Well, that's something we have in common."

My eyes close as sleep draws me in. Time passes in silence.

"Mahlorie?"

Breathe in. Awake. "Yeah?"

"I'm glad it's you. I mean, if I had to have a perfect stranger appear in my head and start to talk to me through my mind, I'm glad the Universe chose you."

Through sleep, I say, "Me too."

And just before radio silence, I hear Dyson whisper, *"For as long as it lasts."*

▫▫ ALONE ▫▫

There are times when I forget that Dyson is in my head and I think I'm alone. It's not a conscious thought. I don't remember he's there. It's a kind of new phenomenon, ya know? Saturday morning is one of those days.

I spend the week avoiding Philip like the plague, because, well, he *is* a plague, and Dad comes home Sunday, so I want to clean the house. Headphones on, I sweep, mop, and dust the house, belt whatever tune pops up on my playlist—and I don't sing well at all— just to piss Philip off, who wears a perma-scowl since I refuse to even look in his direction. With my parents gone, I don't have to put on a polite show. I can treat him exactly how I think of him: non-existent.

Shai calls and I take a break to talk. I want to tell her about Dyson, who I've talked to almost nonstop since our middle of the night conversation. But how do you tell anyone, even your best friend, that you hear a voice in your head and the voice hears you back?

"How are you'?" Shai asks, coolly. "Haven't

67

talked in a few days."

"Sorry. The house is a wreck and I want to get it straightened before Dad gets home."

"Will he be home Sunday?"

"You know me too well. Plus, I've been stuck here alone with Philip, who thinks it's my responsibility to keep him company."

"God, I'm sorry. He ask about me?"

"Of course."

"Recite any good poetry?"

"You know his poetry sucks. But he did leave a note under my door where he'd swapped my name with another girl's. I really think it originally said, 'To Shai'."

We both lose it.

Philip is notorious for writing duplicate love letters to share with multiple girls. Years ago, he had given Shai and me the exact same copy of a letter he'd written, and we'd never let it go. It's too funny. Laughing with my best friend is so easy that the words tumble out my mouth before I can screen. "I met a guy."

Laughter dies. "Oh? Do tell."

No turning back now. But I can't tell her the whole truth. Can I? "His name's Dyson, and he likes to write poetry that doesn't suck."

"That's it? That's all you've got for me?"

"What do you want to know?"

"Everything! What school does he go to? Is he cute? How'd you meet? Why haven't you told me about him?"

"Because it just happened, and well, nothing's happened." Head spins. "He's a guy I've been talking to for a couple weeks. Since after Lucas's party.

Since after the lightning bolt fried my brain.

"A couple weeks? I thought we were best friends." I hear her voice change, but she's more curious than upset as she says, "That's why you've been distant. Busy keeping this guy off my radar, huh? Does he go to our school?"

"No. He's homeschooled."

"Really? How did you meet? Is he cute?"

Deep breath. "He's brilliant and funny and he makes me think, really think, about life and the world and my future. We talk for hours. It's so easy, like we've known each other our whole lives."

Shai giggles. "You know what they call that, don't you? L-O-V-E, Love. You've fallen for this guy."

"No way. I'm not in love with him." Oh, God. I hope he can't hear me.

"Why not?" Shai asks.

"Because we barely know each other," I say.

"So?"

"And we just met."

"And?"

I have no answer. Is she right? It seems so impossible.

"People click, Mal. You don't need a bazillion years to figure it out. Sometimes, you connect with someone for no reason and you feel it, like electricity, that zaps through your whole body whenever you're together. And when he's gone, all you feel is the empty he left behind."

"Feels like Dyson's never gone."

"Totally love. Are you gonna tell me what he looks like or—"

"We haven't met in person yet."

Did I say 'yet'?

"Really?" Shai asks. "Where'd you find this

guy?"

"A…dating site. For people under 18," I lie. "Under18.com."

"Never heard of it. No profile pic?"

"Nope."

"That doesn't concern you?"

"No, Shai. I'm not that superficial."

"That's not even what I meant." I can hear the hurt in her voice.

"What else could it mean?"

Maybe I'm in the wrong here, but I'm sick of so much emphasis placed on appearance. Who cares? But when I imagine his face, it's not hideous. Why do I assume he's cute? What if he's gangly or missing teeth? Would that change how I feel? I'd like to think the answer is no, but I honestly can't say. I know I couldn't bring him home to meet Mom and Dad, that's for sure. Not that I ever would.

"Look, Mal, I'm happy for you. I am. But I want you to be careful. A guy with no profile picture is hiding something. And the fact that you're not even considering that possibility worries me. I love you, and will always support you, but that doesn't mean I won't give you crap when I think you're being stupid, because I know you'd do the same for me."

I smile. "I would. I'm sorry. I love you too."

"I gotta go. Call me later?"

We hang up and I'm drained because I lied to my best friend. I wish I could tell her the details. Then she'd understand. But I can't. I get back to housecleaning, impatient for no reason. I wonder how long this can continue. A boy is in my head and he's unlike anyone I've ever met. I think about him nonstop, and I could talk with him forever.

Then a thought sends a shiver down my spine.

What if this turns off and we can't talk anymore? Emptiness fills me. I'm actually sad. Maybe I do like him more than I admit. This entire situation is irrational and somehow, through it, I've made a connection that I don't want to lose.

But I don't even know Dyson's last name. I don't know where he lives. How are our thoughts transmitted? What if he lives on the other side of the world and we are somehow linked via satellite? Or maybe he lives close by and we can communicate off radio waves...

And it hits me.

"Dyson? You there...Dyson? Hello?" No reply.

Five minutes pass while I call his name. No reply.

I panic.

Where is he? What if he's gone? What if—

"Hey, Mahlorie. You called?"

Relief.

"What took you so long?"

"I was asleep. Sorry."

"No, you don't have to apologize. I got worried, that's all. I thought...we couldn't talk any more. Listen, I think I have an idea why we can hear each other."

"Shoot."

"Do you wear braces?"

"No."

Hope falls. What if the universe gave us this connection for a short while, for some reason we don't know yet, and it will stop as quickly as it started?

"Oh, I thought somehow we'd tapped into a frequency from the metal in our mouths, you know, like a radio signal."

"Good theory."

"Thanks."

"I do have a metal plate in my head."

I sit up. "Seriously?"

"A couple years ago, I was in a real bad car crash and I almost died. Had to put a titanium plate in my head to save my life."

"I almost died a few weeks ago when I was struck by lightning."

"And you wear braces?"

"Uh-huh."

"They titanium?"

"Sure are."

Quiet roars between us.

"Well, it looks like we may have figured out a few connections," Dyson says matter-of-factly. *"We both have metal in our heads and we both almost died. The question becomes why."*

"Why what?"

"Why now? Why us? It can't be simply to talk. Seems an awful lot of effort for the Universe to expel so we can become pen pals."

"What are you saying? Why do you think we can hear each other?"

"I don't know." Dyson sighs. *"But I think maybe it's time we meet. In person."*

▫▫ PRESSURE ▫▫

Panic constricts my chest. I want to run, to hide, but I can't. What am I so afraid of? Lots of people meet for the first time every day and have no idea about the nature or intentions of one another. At least Dyson and I have talked for a while. I flop back on my bed. What scares me most is he could be a great guy.

"Don't be stupid, Mal," Dad's voice cautions. "With a sleight of hand, people can make you see only what they want you to see."

"Be very careful," Mom warns. "People don't really care about who you are until they see that you fit their mold."

My parents battle in my subconscious, like two devils on my shoulders. Their prejudices and misconceptions taught all my life, like Bible School rhetoric, haunt every decision I make, even when they're both hundreds of miles away. What surprises me in this moment is the fact that the panic in my chest isn't my fear that Dyson will reject me.

What if I reject him? "I'm scared," I finally say.

Dyson's nervous laugh disarms me. *Me too. Scared, nervous, excited...so many thoughts run through my head."*

Wish I could hear them. "Like what?" I ask.

"You know...thoughts."

"What, like, do I have warts or three-heads or worse?"

"Actually, more like if you're as beautiful as you sound, then what'll you think of me?"

"I'm not like that."

"As beautiful as you sound?"

I smile as warmth spreads through my chest. "No.

Superficial."

"Oh, so you like warty, three-headedguys?"

"No," I snort.

"What kind of guys do you like?"

I shrug, even though I'm alone. Heartbeat races, mouth suddenly dry. "Smart, funny, not a serial killer." I stare out the window at the bank of storm clouds that roll in. Thunder growls in the distance.

"Two out of three ain't bad. I'm not very funny."

"Shut up! I'm serious."

There's a knock at my door as Dyson rambles on. I shush him before I open it. Phil leans against the doorframe.

"Who you talking to?" He smiles like he's God's gift to the world.

"None of your business. What do you want?"

"Really? I wanted to see if you—"

"Not interested." I close the door in his face. Only his boot stops it.

Evil intentions shine in his eyes. "I wasn't finished." He opens the door and lumbers inside.

"Just get out of my room and stay away from me!"

"I'm done with your games, Mahlorie." He paces my room, and my stomach clenches. "You really haven't been a very good host. I flew all the way here to hang out with my favorite cousin and you've kinda been selfish and rude. I'm over it."

"I'm calling my mother." My phone in hand, I fumble to call Shai before Phil snags it. "Give me my phone back, you jerk!"

"What's going on, Mahlorie?" Dyson shouts in my head.

"Nothing I can't handle."

"Really?" Phil said. "You think you can handle me?"

My breathe held in my throat. "What do you mean, Phil?"

"You know what I mean," he said, stepping took close for my comfort. "I like you, Mal. You know I always have."

"That's disgusting, and you need to back up."

He steps even close, his minty breath in my face. "We're perfect for each other."

"Ew. We're practically family."

Phil smiled. "Only on paper. Not blood relatives."

He grabs my wrists. "Ouch! Stop, Phil. You're hurting me."

"But I really like you, Mal. Always have. And I know you feel the same."

"Let go of me, Phil. I'm serious."

"Get out of there, Mal," Dyson says, *"Whatever it takes. If I was there, I'd hit him with something."*

"Great idea," I say, though Phil takes it as affirmation.

I grab my Junior Magician of the Year trophy

75

off my dresser. I'd won it for making two doves disappear. I hope it can make one snake disappear, too. My fingers brush the cool bronzed metal as Phil's fingers brush my cheek. Once I grip the base, I pull back and smack him in the hand till he lets go, then smack him again as I rush past.

"What's happening? Are you hurt?" Dyson asks, in response to my grunts.

"No. I hit him. Twice."

"Get out of there!"

I grab my phone, sprint downstairs, and out the front door into the cool air, just as the sky releases the first fat raindrops of this storm. Talk about déjà vu.

"Do you have someplace safe to go?"

Tears blend with rain on my cheeks. "I don't know. Shai's, I guess. But it's miles away, and—" A crack of thunder cuts me off. "I won't make it. There's a storm coming, and I don't wanna get struck by lightning again."

"It's storming here, too. We must live kinda close.

But not close enough."

"What do you mean? How can you tell?"

"We caught the tail end of a storm, like the edge, but you seem to be directly in its path."

"Seems to be my luck. So, what do I do?"

"I know this is a crazy question, but do you live anywhere near Beaver's Run?"

"Yeah. My neighborhood backs up to the same woods."

The winds howl while rain pelts me.

"Oh my God, you're in Maverick Estates? That's so crazy. Okay, here's what you're gonna do. Head to the east end exit. There's a dirt path that leads through the woods from there. Take it to about

the halfway point, maybe a little more. My family has a cabin out there. It's in the middle of nowhere, but my family uses it as an escape pod when we want to get out of society and lay low for a while."

"What are you guys, like, in the Mafia?"

"Don't you ever want to unplug? Never mind. We can talk about society's problems another time. Once you pass over the creek, the path forks. Head left, and you'll run right into the place. Got it?"

"Got it."

I dart to the exit, where I'm forced to jump the fence of my gated community. Sure enough, a dirt path runs through the brush and I'm shocked I've never noticed it before. The rain lands like needles, and the wind whips through the trees with a vengeance. Lightning cuts the air as claps of thunder gain. My breaths come ragged.

"I'm right here with you," Dyson reminds me. "Focus on the cabin, and I'll meet you there."

The sky opens overhead and batters me with rain. Lightning puts on a spectacular show with nature's thunderous applause. Puddles form quickly. Water splashes up as I race through the narrow path that weaves through the drenched woods. My bare feet lose grip, my teeth chatter from the cold.

Bright white streaks the sky. The darkened woods illuminate in horror movie effects. Thunder steals my breath. My mind races on what happened in my bedroom. What was he thinking? I fall face first into a muddy hole. Lightning splits a dead oak nearby and it catches fire. I work my eyes open as one of its large limbs crash and the wood burns. I'm propelled to my feet. Shards splinter into fiery rain that embeds in my calves. I yowl in pain and launch forward, unable to respond to Dyson, who screams with concern. I can't take a full breath as another lightning bolt hits the brush beside me, so close static buzzes. Electric shock waves crest out and I'm pushed into a sprint. I've got to get out of here before I'm killed.

Heave—Run—White Light—BOOM! Pant—Tremble—White Light—CRACK!

The path opens on either side as a rush of water swells around me. I cross the bridge, only it's not man- made, as I'd expected. It's a sandbar with a rotten log border whose banks overflow with a flash flood that soaks my path.

Almost there, I tell myself.

A few more yards and I'm wedged back between brush. "Crossed...bridge," I pant.

"You're so close, Mal," Dyson cheers. *"Fork left."*

Within seconds, I reach the fork and shift left, as a fire bolt hits the ground in front of me. I'm launched back through the air until I strike a tree, the wind knocked out of me. My eyes bulge and I can't breathe.

"Mahlorie? Where are you now? Talk to me."

Dyson's muffled voice pierces the resonate ping in my ears.

I lay on my back as water pours down my throat, and I visualize my obituary: *Cause of death: drowned in the woods.* I flip to my side, retch, and gasp until I'm able to manage a few shallow breaths, then finally breathe normally. "I'm okay," I tell Dyson, as I jump to my feet. Only I'm not. A massive, felled tree blocks the path. "Can't get through. There's a tree in the way."

"Can you climb over it?"

"I can't. It's freaking huge." Tears flow. I've

had enough. I swear I will kill Phil myself if I ever make it out of here alive. "I can't see anything. The rain's too heavy. I've got to get out of here!"

"All right," Dyson says. *"You're gonna have to go back to the bridge and jump off the left side, same side as the fork."*

"But aren't there gators and snakes in this water?"

"Yes. But the stream backs up to the cabin. It'll take you right there."

"No way. You're crazy. There's no way I'll jump in that water."

"Mahlorie—"

"One lightning strike anywhere in that water and I'm toast. Dead. I can't. There has to be another way."

"There's not. I wish there were, but if you don't get out of there, from the sound of it, you're gonna be dead either way. That water rises fast, and you don't want to be caught off guard. Trust me. I'm right here with you. You can do this."

Trapped, I groan and backtrack to the bridge, scan the water for predators, but find none. Rain bounces off the surface as the storm passes. Carefully, I cross the rotten logs and slip into the stream, cold from rain. My feet hit the silt bottom and launch off. "I can't do this! I can't." I scramble up the logs.

"Yes, you can. The faster you get through this, the faster you'll be in a dry cabin. Let's go!"

With a nod to no one, I slide back into the ice water, where I cringe as my feet squish into the murky bottom. I try not to imagine what creatures lurk beneath the waist high water I trudge through, as I fight hysterics.

"Listen to my voice," Dyson says. His voice is a calm dream that comforts me. *"Follow my voice. Put one foot in front of the other. Don't be afraid. Each step brings you closer to me. Do you believe that?"*

"Yes," I say, through clenched teeth. The water hits my chest. "Oh, God...it's getting higher."

"Now, move faster. Imagine each step is your last. Stretch your arms out and pull the water out of your way. Throw it behind you. Keep stretching. Keep stepping."

The rain falls in a drizzle that no longer splashes up. Ahead, the stream curves around an unseen bend where a six-foot alligator clings to the opposite shore.

"Oh, my God, Dyson! There's an alligator!"

"Mahlorie, listen to me. Keep stretching. Keep stepping."

"It's moving," I cry. "It's moving!"

"Listen to my voice. Shut it all out, except my voice. I won't let anything happen to you. Do you trust me?"

My voice shakes, but I whisper, "Yes," as the gator moves steadily closer.

"Have you passed the old dock yet?"

"I don't know." I can hardly think.

"It'll be some posts that jut up. You could mistake it for underwater logs, except they're positioned too perfect to be natural."

My eyes scan the banks in search of a needle in a... "Yeah, I see them. I'm passing it."

"Good. Up ahead the stream's gonna narrow some, but right after that, you'll see the beach that leads to the cabin."

"How long?" The gator slinks uncomfortably close.

"Seconds."

The banks squeeze close and the trees draw together like curtains in the finale.

"Dy-son…"

"Any second."

"Oh, God…"

"Keep stretching. Keep stepping."

The gator will close the gap between us any minute. I pray lightning strikes me first. That I know I might survive.

Distant thunder rumbles.

The storm is too far away to save me. The gator looms closer.

Teeth chatter painfully. Blackness surrounds.

"Stretch-step. Stretch-step."

I'm not gonna make it.

And as the thought enters my mind, the beach appears as a welcome mat that I scurry across until I reach the back door of the cabin and I'm safe inside. I collapse in a soaked heap on the hardwood floor.

"Safe."

▫▫ TRUST ▫▫

It's dark in Dyson's musty cabin, and I don't move until I really believe I'm safe. Tendrils of lightning streak the sky as rain hammers the roof, then seeps through the space between the logs. I'm drenched through and through, my teeth chatter out of control, and my cell phone is long gone.

"Dyson, you there?"

"Always. You okay?"

"Cold, wet, but alive thanks to you."

"You're the one who did it. I only kept you company."

I grin. "Okay, now how about you guide me to the lights. I can't see in here."

"They're by the front door, through the kitchen."

Boards moan with each wet footstep I take. My toes bump an area rug. The fibers scratch my battered soles and I smack into a chair my outstretched hands missed. Lightning strobes offer glimpses of my surroundings until I finally reach the front door and find the light switch. But when I click it on, nothing happens.

"No electricity," I say wearily.

"Look on the other side of the door."

I shimmy my hand across the smooth wood, find another panel, and hallelujah. Let there be light!

The bungalow is adorable with sparse furnishings, oil painted nature scenes that make me cringe after what I've just lived through, and frilly country curtains above each window. A large-mouth bass hangs proudly over the mantle, its glass eyes trained on me.

"Much better. Where's the bathroom? And a towel?"

"Towel's in the bathroom. Are you short or tall?"

"Excuse me?"

"My mom's tiny, like a small. I thought you could borrow some of her clothes."

"I'll let mine dry." No way I'll wear his mom's clothes. "I'll let you know when I'm done."

Radio silence.

I reach the bathroom, strip down, and jump into a shower that's icy till the end. Beads of water fall while I stare at the tile. It's weird how quickly Dyson goes offline. It's as if he really does only talk when I listen. I never hear him otherwise. I don't know how I'd feel if he shushed me up then let me know when he was ready to talk.

My seared calves don't look as bad as I expect. I find some tweezers, ointment, and a bandage in the medicine cabinet. The splintered wood takes a painful minute to come out, before I discharge myself, wrapped in a soft towel, a million times better. I cross to the nearest room and open the door where stale air rushes out. Dark blue walls, walnut furniture, fishing poles and nets, and a guitar in the corner. Pictures line the dresser beneath a mirror where my bruised reflection stares at me. In the frames, a young, dark-haired boy smiles with his mom and dad at a theme park. That same boy a few years older holds the large-mouth bass from the mantle at the end of a fishing line. His eyes sparkle in the same grayish-blue color as the sea behind him.

"I think I've found your room," I tell Dyson, "and damn you were a cute kid!"

"Not fair."

"Why not?" No response. "That's what I thought." A photo near the end catches my eye. It's Dyson quite a few years older. Angular lines have replaced baby fat. Dimples have deepened around his smile. Lips invite a kiss... "You shaved your hair?"

"You're still in my room?"

"Get over it. Why'd you shave your hair? This a recent picture of you?"

"I was fourteen and it was taken three summers ago in Sarasota on vacation. Now stop snooping."

"I'm not snooping," I say absently, as my fingers brush across his stormy sea eyes. Dark eyelashes fan beneath prominent brows. Freckles pepper the bridge of his nose. He doesn't look at all as I've imagined. He is drop-dead gorgeous! Suddenly, I'm nervous and self- conscious. What will he think of me when he sees me for the first time? I'm not Shai. I'm not beautiful or exotic. This guy's in a whole different league than me.

"So, what do you think?"

"What?" I drop the photo.

"I know it's an old picture, but do I look at all like you thought I would? Same hair color or eye color you expected?"

"Oh, well...it's hard to tell that stuff from a

voice, you know?"

"Just as I expected."

"What?"

"I'm not your type, am I?"

"No, it's not that at all. I mean, I don't have a type, but you're not—*not* it." What's the matter with me? I sound like an idiot. *Get it together, Mahlorie. This is Dyson. You're the one who always says appearance doesn't matter.* Usually, scolding myself helps to put my world in perspective. Not so much when I can't say it out loud.

"I like the way you look," I manage. "A lot."

"You do?"

"But even if I didn't, it wouldn't matter, right?"

"And why's that?"

Butterflies battle in my gut. What happened? I go from a near death experience to an emotional outburst, like I'm in some old Sandra Bullock movie or something. "Would it matter to you? What if I'm not your type? What if I look different than you expect?"

"Not possible."

I grunt. "Of course, it is. How can you say that?"

In a softened voice, Dyson says, *"Your hair, curly or straight, dark or light, would still force my eyes closed if it brushed my skin. Your body, large or small, would still feel warm pressed against mine. Your eyes...well, I'd get lost in them regardless of their shape or color."*

My breath stammers as his words caress me. "How can you know?"

"Mahlorie, you're beautiful. Your mind, your heart. That's why I can't wait to talk with you every day. Your voice...your laugh. Your courage. How

could your appearance ever change those feelings? That's how I know. That's why it doesn't matter."

Warmth spreads out from my stomach. I think I'm falling in love with this boy. "Dyson?"

"Yes?"

"Can you come stay with me tonight?"

"Mal, I wish I could, but I don't have any way to get—"

"No, I mean, can you stay with me in my mind? I don't want to be alone."

"Always. Give me a sec."

While I wait, I shake off the comforter that covers Dyson's bed and snuggle beneath it. The pillowcase lingers with the scent of soap and musk. This must be what he smells like. As I soak in his aroma, a satisfied grin spreads across my face.

"Mal? You there?"

"Yup. Not going anywhere tonight."

"I wish more than anything in the world that I could be right there with."

"Me too."

He let out a held breath. *"Now, since I will eventually fall asleep, I'm gonna put on some headphones and play music all night. That way anytime you wake up, you'll know I'm here with you. And if you wanna talk, say something."*

"Thank you, Dyson. I'm really glad it's you too…in my head."

"Goodnight, Mal."

"Night."

Music soars faintly in my ears, and I'm comforted he's with me. I close my eyes, breath in his scent, in his bed, his beautiful face in my mind's eye, until sleep draws me away.

▫▫ COMIC ▫▫

When I open my eyes, every inch of my body aches in protest. I moan and stretch.

Dyson is quick to say, *"Morning, sunshine. How do ya feel today?"*

"Like I wrestled a gator and lost."

"Ouch!"

Through a yawn, I add, "You should see the gator." I search for a clock but come up empty. "What time is it?"

"Almost ten."

Adrenaline punches me awake. "Are you serious? Oh my God." I jump up and cringe when my sore feet take on my weight. "I gotta get out of here."

"Why? What's the rush? It's Sunday."

"My dad's home today from a business trip. He'll be worried sick if I'm not there. And who knows what story Philip will spin him?" My towel molts to the floor, and I put on my swamp-water-starched clothes I'd left to dry on the chairs. They smell something awful. "How do I get out of here, Dyson?"

"You headed home?"

"No way. Not until I know that creep's gone

for good."

"Then where to?"

"Ponce Landing. It's where Shai lives."

"You could come to my place. I'm not far from Shai's."

I hesitate. "I can't. This is bad enough as it is, and I'm sure my dad would have a heart attack if I added a *guy-two-years-older-than-me-whose-bed-I'd-spent-the-night-in* to the equation."

"Heard and understood."

"So, can you walk me out of here or what?"

"With my eyes closed."

"Funny."

"Ah, finally. Three for three."

We laugh as I get ready and head out the front door. A tinge of guilt like a tiny bell resounds as my fingertips brush the picture I've stolen from Dyson's bedroom and hidden in my pocket.

□□□□□

Dyson has an uncanny way to make me forget my surroundings.

It takes over an hour to trudge barefoot through the muddy forest to the road that leads to Shai's neighborhood. I mostly listen as Dyson shares the history of DC Comics. Superman. The Flash. Batman. Their beginning, their legacies, and the intricacies that surround them.

"They always have a weakness, you know? Like the gods of Greece and Rome, yet they were able to overcome them through acts of valor and heroism to save those weaker than them."

"Kind of like you," I say.

"I don't know about that."

"You're my hero. You saved my life."

"Maybe we've saved each other," Dyson continues, a smile evident in his lilt. *"Interestingly, the villains also have weaknesses, and theirs are usually the same as the heroes, at least in their own minds."*

"How do you mean?" I ask, as I skate the pebbled barrier that borders the two-lane highway.

"Well, Batman's weakness is those he loves. His whole mission is to protect the citizens of Gotham because no one was there to protect him when his parents were murdered right in front of him. He makes it his job, his life's work, to fight crime. He is led by his heart, even when it takes him to people like Selina Kyle."

"Who?"

"Catwoman."

"Halle Berry or Michelle Pfeiffer?"

Dyson chuckles. *"Neither. Catwoman is more of an anti-hero than a true villain, more Batman's female nemesis. Although she's portrayed as a lover, maybe even the greatest of all of them, she's a thief by trade, which puts her among the garbage of Gotham, exactly who Batman fights against. But she's also an animal activist, and most of her moves are based off either saving animals, funding that cause, or attacking those who she feels have done the opposite.*

"The difference is that Batman brings justice to Gotham while Catwoman works out of her need for revenge. She doesn't want to help others, she wants to help herself, regardless of what she has to do to get there. Sure, she has a strict moral code and doesn't kill, which is one of the reasons Batman lets her slip through the cracks on more than one occasion. And because he falls in love with her.

Love can make you do things you wouldn't normally do."

"How do you know all this stuff?"

"Trust me, I spend a lot of time reading comics."

I smile as I enter Shai's neighborhood. "So, which are we, heroes or villains? I mean we've got this freak power or curse. It depends on how you look at it."

"It's definitely not a curse," Dyson says. His curved lips tempt even in my mind's eye. Shivers pulse through my body despite the wretched heat. *"No matter how long it lasts, I know it's been a gift to meet you. To get inside your head."*

"Trust me, you don't want to stay there too long. Plus you're the first guy who can actually make that claim."

"Why don't you let people in?"

Suddenly the air becomes stagnant. I'm on Shai's street, her house about a dozen or so up ahead on the right. The sun beats relentlessly, and a burn settles across my freckled nose. I picture my mother, my father. Phil. "Lots of reasons."

"Go ahead. I'm listening."

"Don't remind me."

"I'm serious. Why are you so guarded?"

"Honestly, because most people I've met are like your comic book villains, only they portray themselves as the heroes." Sweat becomes a second layer of skin, and I'm so thirsty I can barely swallow. Luckily, Shai's house is around the bend. "People are fake. My parents. My friends. Reality TV. I don't have time for fake. Not now, not tomorrow, not ever."

"Okay, soapbox. I get it. Sorry I asked."

My pulse pounds a headache across my skull. "No. Sorry, it's hot. I'm tired and thirsty."

"You never need to apologize to me. I'm not easily offended. Thick skin." He pauses and clears his throat. *"So, what's Shai like? How'd you two become friends?"*

"Shai's great. She's popular and beautiful and when no one's around has the biggest heart in the whole world. I hate how she dumbs herself down because she thinks that's what'll make her popular. She's way smarter than she lets on, even though she always gives me crap for being such a nerd."

"So, what keeps you friends then? You sound very different."

"We are, but in the same sense we really fill in each other's weaknesses." I glimpse Shai's pale-yellow house and get my second wind. "Plus, she's brutally honest with me. No matter how I take it. And she's always been there for me."

"Did you tell her about me?"

"Sort of."

"Oh, I gotta hear this. What did you tell her? There's a boy stuck in my head and I can't get rid of him?"

"Kind of left that part out. I told her what I thought about you and that you were homeschooled..."

"And?"

I reach her driveway. White spots jump in and out of my vision. "And...she asked where you lived and how we met."

"Is this where you told her we met in your head?"

"No. I told her we met on a dating site...for under eighteen-year-olds. Under18.com."

Dyson's gasp and laughter make me laugh back.

"Shut up! Did she believe you?"

"What was I supposed to tell her?"

Dyson stutters between belly laughs. *"I'm sorry, Mal. I am. Did she buy it?"*

"No, but she didn't ask any more questions but told me to be careful." I struggle to take in a full breath. I've got to get into some AC.

"That's good advice, considering. You really are one of a kind."

"I'm at her door, so you've got to get out of my head, okay?"

Laughter dies. *"All right. But before I go, will you promise me one thing?"*

"Sure. Anything."

Doorbell rings.

Head spins.

"If this frequency were to cut off and not come back, promise me you won't come and look for me."

Tunnel vision.

"Won't come and look for you?" I mumble. Wide eyes.

Air's hot.

Darkness floods my view. "Dyson?"

No noise. Panic. "Don't. Go."

The front door is opened by Shai's mom. My eyes trail skyward, and the sun briefly chases the darkness away. But it returns and overcomes, with big red spots in its wake as I collapse on the stoop.

□□□□□

I awaken in a cool, dark room that's not my own. Posters of shirtless boys line the pastel walls and I instantly know I'm in Shai's bedroom. My lips are cracked. My throat, sand. Head pounds lightly, the headache a faint memory. A glass of water on the nightstand goes down before I take a breath. I've never been so thirsty in all my life. My eyes want to close, but the door opens, and light sweeps the room.

"Hey, Mal. How do you feel?" Shai asks in a whisper.

"Like death."

She sits beside me. "You don't look too hot."

"Thanks."

"Or smell too hot."

I glare at her as best I can till we both smile. "What happened to you?" Shai pushes dark hair from my eyes.

"Long story. I'll explain later. Right now, I've got to talk to my dad."

"He's on his way here now. With Phil."

I gasp, bolt upright, and seethe, "No! He can't come here." A wave of nausea rises, but I push it down. "Not Phil." My eyes water. "Shai, he freaked out last night. Busted into my room and wouldn't leave."

"What? Oh, my God. Why didn't you call me?"

"The jerk took my phone when I said I was gonna call Mom, when I was actually gonna call you, and then he grabbed my wrists...hard. It was awful. I was so scared." My tears soak Shai's shoulder.

"Aw, sweetie. I'm so sorry. How'd you get away?"

"I clocked him with a trophy. Then got out of the house. It was horrible."

"Why didn't you come here?"

93

"It was too far, especially in the storm."

"So, then where'd you stay?"

My eyes widen. "Shai, listen to me. I need you to get your mom to tell my dad that I spent the night here, okay?"

"Mahl-or-ie. What happened?"

"I swear, I will tell you every tiny detail. But please, go talk to your mom. Tell her he was drunk, and I was afraid to go home or whatever you need for her to understand."

"You want me to get my mom to lie to your dad?"

"Yes."

She stares until her curiosity wins out. "Okay. But you're gonna owe me. Big time."

"I know."

Shai heads for the door. "Every juicy detail about your night with—what's his name again?"

"Dyson."

"I'm right here, Mahlorie," Dyson says.

Shai leaves.

"Mal? You there?"

I don't respond to him.

The truth is, after the promise Dyson asked me to keep, I'm not sure I'm ready to talk to him yet. Maybe he's not the hero I thought he was. Maybe he's my anti- hero. I close my eyes, listen to him call my name, until he swears at me and finally falls silent. A tear rolls to my pillow as I close my eyes, beg sleep to come, but find only dark, empty silence.

PART TWO

The Curse

▫▫ NORMAL ▫▫

There's a reason people say don't mess with a mama bear's cubs.

I have never in all my life seen my mother so infuriated as she was after Dad told her what had happened with Philip. Since Dad didn't want to see me grow up with a mom behind prison bars, he put Philip on the first plane out, like *do-not-pass-go-do-not-collect-$200.00* kind of out, and I stayed at Shai's until the smoke cleared. True to her word, her mom lied to my parents, although I had to tell her the truth. Well, most of it. I told her about Dyson and his parent's cabin and how we'd met online, and she was okay with those parts. I did have to lie about how I used my cell phone till it got too wet to get to the cabin before I lost it. But she believed me enough to let it go.

Mom put her schedule on hold to play the role of my shadow. I mean, she drives me to school and back, wants to have "girl time," which means two completely different things to each of us. She literally follows me around everywhere I go in attempts to "bond." We're at DiBella's Ice Cream Parlor at least twice a week. I can't take it anymore!

But every night, before I go to bed, I take out Dyson's picture and stare at it. The curves of his lips. His square jaw. And his eyes are two oceans that disappear into a horizon beyond my grasp. I know he's in my head, but I can't bring myself to mention the promise he asked me to keep. Not yet.

Thankfully, three weeks after Phil is kicked out, homelife starts to resemble normalcy. Mom's glued to her phone, Dad's out on a ship telling stale jokes that still somehow get laughs, and I'm back to plain old Mahlorie, the girl unnoticed. Mom resumes her schedule and leaves in two days. No more drunk neighbors or psycho relatives alone with me. I wish they'd let me stay by myself, but both my parents were hellraisers who have sworn I will never have an opportunity to throw a party while they're gone, like their parents gave them so freely.

They really don't know me at all.

This time, I'm at Shai's house. Our moms don't exactly get along, which is funny because they are so alike in so many ways. They're both aloof when it comes to parenting while both believe they're the greatest mothers in the universe. And ironically, they both judge the others "compromised moral code" although my mom makes her living writing about women just like Shai's mom.

Before Mom leaves, I have an appointment with Dr. Ant Killer, which sucks, except that it'll get me out of school tomorrow. But today, I'm in class, in English to be exact, as Mr. Charron, the hottest teacher in school, discusses "The Masque of the Red Death," a Poe classic.

"The beauty of this story," he says, as he flips dark hair from his eyes, "is Poe's elegant use of symbolism. Here you have this echelon of society desperate to hide from death within the walls of Prince Prospero's elaborate abbey. But to up the wow factor, as if it needed it, he's painted seven rooms with seven different colors in unison. The sofas, the curtains, the carpets, you name it." He stops. "What do you think these colors stood for, and why the different colored light in the black room only?"

Silence swarms loudly as eyes avert Mr. Charron, as if he's the Red Death himself. Annoyed, my hand lifts.

"Yes, Mahlorie?"

"Maybe the different ways we see ourselves as people. You know, like, blue is calming and red means anger. Stuff like that."

"So different facets of the human psyche?" He perches on a stool, toned legs flex beneath tight jeans.

"Yeah, I guess. Except the red on black. That's totally a symbol of blood and death."

"It's interesting that Poe would choose doors and rooms to represent completely different feelings and emotions, as if to show the competition underway in our minds as we navigate through life to avoid Death." Mr. Charron continues as the debate heightens, though I no longer listen, since Dyson whispers,

"'Masque of the Red Death,' right? Poe classic."

A grin spreads the width of my face, and I grunt to let him know A) I'm in class, and B) he's correct.

He adds, *The worst truth in that story is that Death can't be avoided and often times comes masked totally different then our expectations.*

"Kinda morbid," I muster.

"You wanna read a real mind screw?" Dyson says, *"Read 'The Monkey's Paw.' That story will mess you up."*

"Tell me," I whisper through cupped hands.

"Well, there's a monkey's paw and it's able to grant wishes, so this guy wishes he was rich, right, only to get a knock on the door that his son died a gruesome death in the factory's machinery system. Then, he wishes for his son back, only what's coming isn't really his son anymore."

"Gross. Does he make it back?"

"No. The guy's final wish is for his son to be at peace." Dyson's voice trails—drifts, as if he's lost in thought.

This is the most we've talked in weeks and one of the few times when he's the one who reaches out to me first. It's my fault, of course. I still haven't found the courage to ask him why he said not to look for him, in case, you know…. But the truth is—

The bell rings.

In the noise and commotion, I tell him, "I miss you."

"I miss you too. More than you know."

Before I leave class, I whisper, "I need to talk to you after school, okay?"

"Sure. You know where to find me."

And he's gone.

ooooo

The day drags, each class painstakingly long and oh, so boring. At the final bell, I rush off campus to walk home, when I see Mom's black Explorer parked along the curb. My shoulders hunch as she flags me over. Two more days and she'll be far away and neglectful again. I can't wait. Honestly, this *Mom of the Year* stuff has started to tick me off.

I jump in the car, greeted by Mom's sweet perfume and ice-cold AC. Her manicured hand covers mine. "Hey, lambkin. How was your day?"

"Fine."

She turns down the positive affirmation CD and faces me. "That's it? Fine?"

"Yeah," I say, eyebrows raised. "You went to high school. Pretty much the same waste of time now as it was then."

She feigns disapproval. "Now, Mahlorie, I'm sure that's not true. You must be the topic of the year with all that you've been through lately."

I glare at her. "I'm not a character in your book, *Victoria.*"

She puts the car into gear. "Please, don't call me that. You know I dislike it."

"Then don't analyze my life like you're plotting it for some stupid book you're gonna write, okay?" Anger rises so quickly, I wonder where it comes from. Still, I mean every word. I will not apologize.

After several minutes, Mom says, "Obviously, I've upset you."

"Obviously," I mimic, as I stare out the window and wish I were anyone else but me.

"Well, that wasn't my intention. Really, Mahlorie, I can't for the life of me understand your animosity toward me."

I roll my eyes, though she can't see.

"I'm trying my best to juggle a successful career while being a good mother. And I know I don't always get it right, but if you'd cut me some slack every now and then..." Her words trail. A pang of guilt crests in my stomach. "What I mean is you are more important to me than anything else. What happened with Philip was horrible. None of us could have known that he was capable of..."

Her voice trembles as if on the verge of tears. I face her profile.

"I'm sorry, Mahlorie. I wish I could go back and rewrite it, like I can a scene in a book. But I can't. I can't plot you like one of my characters, though I sometimes wish I could. Real life is much messier than fiction." I smile, almost sorry for my mother after her confession, until she adds, "Sometimes, it's easier to kill off a character and simply start over."

And with that, my smile disappears, and we ride home in silence.

ooooo

Shai's texts hit before I even walk through the door. I grab a snack, head upstairs to do homework, and read her message.

Good news Party Friday!

I text back: NO.

My new phone rings. "What do you mean 'NO'?"

"No, Shai. I mean I'm not going to another stupid party with you. Did you forget what happened the last time?"

"Whatever, you totally owe me."

"How do you figure?"

"My mom lied to your dad. Game on."

My head drops between my legs. I knew that

was gonna come back and bite me.

"And this time, no twins. Those guys were total creeps. They won't even be there. I swear to God. It's not even a party, really, more of a get-together. Lucas and a couple of his friends and their girlfriends."

"Sounds great," I say, as I open my backpack. "So that'd make me, what, the fifth wheel? Maybe the seventh?"

"No, you have a boyfriend now. You can bring … God, why can't I ever remember his name?"

"Dyson?"

"Yes," both Dyson and Shai chime in unison.

"I don't think so, Shai. He's not going."

"He's not going where?" Dyson asks.

"No," I whisper.

"What do you mean, no? You invite Dyson, and he comes to Lucas's get-together, if for no other reason than to prove that he's not a figment of your imagination."

I nearly drop the phone. If she only knew. "Fine. I'll ask him."

"Ask me what?" Dyson says.

I ignore him.

"Perfect," Shai beams. "Then it's a date."

We hang up, and I take a deep breath before I ask Dyson, "You feel like going to a party with me Friday?"

And the world stops when he answers, *"Yes."*

▫▫ REPEAT ▫▫

Friday morning, I sit in the waiting room at Dr. Ant Killer's office. I wish I'd brought a sweatshirt. I flip through the pages of a fashion magazine to kill time, but quickly realize I'd rather sit and freeze to death than subject myself to "Six Ways to Tell if He's Really into You." Okay, I'm not gonna lie. That one piques my interest.

I turn to the quiz. *Question One: Does he go out of his way to be with you?* Hmmmm. I guess a boy stuck in your head makes that a yes, but I guess we'll see tonight. *Question Two: Is he the talker or the listener?* Funny, but I seem to be the one who initiates most of the conversations, though his stupid comment has slowed that up. *Question Three: Does he keep you at a distance or make you feel like the only person in the world?* This one strikes home. Sometimes, I feel like it's Dysonville, population two.

I toss the magazine, lumber into the bathroom, and close the door behind me. "Dyson?"

"Yes?"

Without. Skipping. A beat. "You busy?" I ask.

"Never for you."

Why is this so difficult? Come on, Mahlorie.

Get a grip!

"Why'd you tell me not to look for you?"

Silence.

This boy is killing me. And it's not even that question that I really want the answer to. I don't wait for his response. Instead I go in for the real answer I'm afraid to hear. "Do you like me still? I mean, are you only talking to me because we're stuck like this?"

There. I said it.

"No," he says, as the receptionist calls my name.

"No what?" I say. "No, you don't like me anymore?"

"No."

"No?"

"Mahlorie, will you shut up and let me talk?"

The receptionist calls me again, irritated because she thinks I told her no.

"Yes, I still like you," he says. *"I'm crazy about you. And I love talking with you, no matter how infrequent."*

"Then why'd you say that?"

"It's complicated."

"This whole situation is complicated," I blurt out. "And when you tell me not to look for you if—"

"I don't want you to get hurt."

That shuts me up.

Now, the receptionist knocks at the door impatiently. "Ms. Moore, you need to come out now."

"One minute," I call, as I flush the unused toilet and turn on the faucet to buy time. "How could finding you get me hurt?" I ask Dyson.

"I don't know. A feeling, okay?"

"You are still coming tonight, right?"

"Of course. It'll be our Cyrano de Bergerac moment."

"Huh?" More impatient knocks. "Coming," I holler, and turn off the faucet.

"I'll explain tonight. I can't wait to finally see you in person."

"Me too, but I gotta go. This lady's gonna blow if she has to call me in to see the dentist for much longer."

He's gone before I open the door.

I'm greeted by the stern, displeased face of the receptionist who leads me to the exam room. I'm surprised I'm not chained like a prisoner and dragged behind her. *Dead girl walking.* Her personality, like her starched hair, has no give. She closes the door behind her as she leaves. Reclined in my chair, I smile. I'm gonna meet Dyson tonight. I can't believe it. Nerves grow into cold shivers. I can't keep still. I take deep breaths and close my eyes. His beautiful face and calm suddenly cover me like oil. The door creaks and my eyes bolt open.

Dr. Ant Killer, with his tanned face, Ken doll hair, and flashy white smile. "Well, hello, Mahlorie. How are we today?"

"Good," I answer.

"Excellent." He sits on the swivel stool beside me. "Any problems with your braces?"

I shake my head. He slides on gloves and adjusts the hover lamp. Instruments prod, poke, and yank my head in violent thrusts. He pushes the light away. "Your mouth looks well-taken care of, and you'll be excited to know that your braces are ready to come off."

Oh God, that's today? He can't take them off now. What if I lose my connection with Dyson? I still

10

don't know enough about him. How can I stall this?

"Are you sure they're ready to come off? I mean I'd hate for you to rush the job and my teeth end up crooked again. A whole lot of wasted time, you know what I mean? We could wait another week."

He stares at me, sits back on his swivel seat, and says, "I know what the problem is."

"You do?" I say, confused.

"I do. You're worried about how people will look at you without your braces, aren't you?"

I force a grin. "Sure. That's exactly what I'm afraid of. Too much pressure."

Dr. Ant Killer grins back. "You're fine, Mahlorie. You will have a glowing smile, and people will love it. Believe me, you're not the first patient to go from hating braces to feeling like they need them."

Only, I do need them.

"Now sit back," he says. "This won't take long." My head hits the rest, my mouth opens too wide, and bright hot light assaults me. One last time, Dr. Ant Killer works on my brackets, which brings tears to my closed eyes. My mouth doesn't hurt, but my heart breaks. I'm about to lose Dyson forever. How could I be so stupid and not get his number? I know I asked for it, but then we start to talk about something else and never get back to phone numbers. Nothing I can do about it now. Can't even say goodbye.

About halfway through, Dr. Ant Killer stops and asks, "Do you hear that?"

"Hear what?" I ask though it's more like "'ear 'ut?"

"I don't know." He leans his ear toward my pried opened mouth.

Oh, my God. Dyson must have his headphones

in.

"What is that?" Dr. Ant Killer says.

I shake my head as if to tell him I don't hear it.

"That hum. You don't hear it?"

"Uh-uh," I say.

Dr. Ant Killer touches my braces with his instrument and, like an amp, the buzz swells into nearly audible music. This is not good. Dr. Ant Killer pulls the instrument back and the music dies. He repeats it over and over. "It almost sounds like music. You really don't hear it? This is phenomenal."

I shake my head, and the pointed tip of the tool in his hand catches in a groove and rips my bracket free. Suddenly, the music stops. Then, I feel pain, taste blood, and utter a screech.

"Are you all right?" Dr. Ant Killer asks. "Let me take a look."

I shake my head as he pries my mouth wider and shoves in a mirrored instrument. "Looks like it barely nicked your cheek." He takes the tool out and stares at me. "Your mouth and head seem to bleed more than the rest of your body, but I promise, it's only a scratch." He washes his hands and dries them with a paper towel. "You seem on edge today, and I don't think it's safe for me to continue with the procedure. We'd be better off to reschedule. It will give you time to let the idea of life without braces sink in."

He loosens the equipment, so I can close my mouth and adds, "Unfortunately, I'll have to replace the bracket that broke. Let me see if I have this type in the back. Be back in one moment." He stands and leaves the room.

I let out a long-held sigh. It's a miracle, my third in a few short weeks, if you count surviving a lightning strike and telecommunication with an unknown boy. Alone, I whisper, "Dyson? Dyson, can you hear me?"

No response.

No music.

No sound.

"Dyson? You there?"

There's a rap on the door, then it opens. Dr. Ant Killer holds a new bracket inside a small box. I open my mouth and he gets to work. "There. That should do the trick. Hopefully, this will stop that buzz sound as well. Have a great weekend."

"You too."

He leaves, and I pray that it worked.

"Dyson? Can you hear me?"

Radio Silence. No channels. Flatline.

It didn't work. He isn't there. It's too soon. I'm not ready to lose him. There has to be a way to reconnect us, to get us both back on the same frequency. What if this new bracket isn't made from titanium? I need to find the broken one. I scan the floor on all fours till I find it. I slip it into my pocket.

"Dyson," I try again. "Please be messing with me." But he's gone.

And all I can feel is the empty he left behind.

▫▫ FACE OFF ▫▫

Shai tells her mom we're headed to the movies as a car pulls up in the driveway.

"Have fun," she yells absently. "Bye, Mom," Shai yells as we leave.

As the door closes behind me, my gaze lands on the green car parked in the driveway. I freeze.

"Listen, Mal," Shai pleads, "I know what you're thinking. And—"

"I am not going with them." I twist around, reach for the doorknob.

Shai grabs my wrist. "I would've told you sooner."

"But you knew I wouldn't go."

We stew in silence.

The driver's side window opens. "You want a ride or not?" Jake asks.

"Yes," Shai hollers, as I yell, "No."

She grabs my hand. "Please, Mal. It's a ride. Otherwise, I can't see Lucas and you won't meet Dyson. I promise this will never happen again."

I know she means her promise. I also know she can't keep it.

The truth is I do want to see Dyson, so I let out

a dramatic sigh and say, "Fine."

□□□□□

In front of Lucas's house sit four parked cars. I guess it really is a small get-together. Jake stops against the curb, and Shai thanks him for the ride before they drive off.

"Where're they headed?" I ask.

She shrugs, aloof.

Inside, voices trickle down from upstairs. I climb behind Shai, where we hang a left to follow the curved hallway till it opens at a large game room. A flat screen television hangs like a painting. Pool and air hockey tables cover half the room, and several dart boards line the far wall. Two couches face each other, upholstered in a deep, forest green leather that matches the drapes and accents in the area rug. The room is massive.

"Wanna drink?" Shai hands me a Solo cup.

"What is it?" I ask.

"Kool Aid. Just drink it."

I take a sip. Whatever it is, they mixed too much sugar to mask the taste. I set my cup down, not interested. I know everyone in the room from school, but I'm not really friends with them. Time to mingle. I grip my red cup, make small talk, listen in on conversations, and play a game of darts with Shai. After a while, Lucas says it's time to watch a movie and passes out popcorn he made in one of those machines like they have in the movie theaters.

Shai comes over. "It's movie time. Where's your boyfriend?

"I don't know."

"Well, you should call him."

"Oh…good idea." I fumble in my bag for my phone, realize I don't have a number for him. "I'm gonna go downstairs and call him, where it's quiet, and probably wait for him on the porch, okay?"

"You sure? I can come hang with you if you want."

"No, you're here with Lucas. Don't worry about me."

"You're my best friend. I always worry about you."

I hate when I lie to Shai, but I can't tell her the truth. And if I say what I feel out loud, I know I'll break into tears. Where is he? Did he ditch? Is he grateful we can't talk anymore and finally able to break ties with me? My heart aches as I hug Shai and hurry down the stairs two at a time. The house quiets. The upstairs light dims as the movie begins. I slip silently out the front door. What am I supposed to do? I can't call him. I can't talk to him at all anymore. A porch swing hangs on the far corner and I climb onto it, gently push off the wooden planks. A million stars fill what sky I see. Crickets chirp through the humid air. The rock lulls me.

A car door closes, and my eyes shoot open. I must've fallen asleep. Nerves alert, I scan for Dyson and jump to my feet. Instead, Tweedle-Dumb and Tweedle-Dumber return with more beer than they could possibly drink before the night ends, although I'm sure they'll give it their best shot. Idiots. Once again, I'm with Shai where my ride gets drunk. I check the time: 11:17 pm. *Where is he? This is ridiculous.*

I stand as the front door opens.

"Hey," Shai says. "You're still out here? Everything okay?"

11

"No," I say. "Everything is not okay."

"Where's Dyson?"

"No idea."

"Did you call him?"

"No reception."

"Really? My phone works fine."

"Not on my end. His."

"Oh."

"I'm over it. If he wants to stand me up, I'm not gonna chase him down." But Shai knows me.

"Oh, sweetie." She hugs me, and I hold back tears. "It's his loss. Can't trust the internet. It's gonna be all right."

With a nod, I wipe my eyes and try to compose myself.

"Why don't you come inside?" she asks. "Not really up to it."

"You wanna go home?"

"No, no," I say, calmly. "Go have fun. Don't worry about me. I'll be fine. I just need a few minutes."

"You sure? It's really no big deal."

I grin. "I'm good."

"I love you," she says. "You're my best friend in the whole world."

"You too," I say.

She goes back inside. I stare at the ground. What did I do wrong? Why doesn't he want to see me? Even if he showed now, I'm so hurt I don't know if I will wait for him. Better to be active than reactive, right? I decide yes and slip into the house as quietly as possible. I hear laughter from upstairs and wish so badly that I could fit in and be a part of the normalcy, hang with a group of friends, watch a movie, and feel like a part of the group instead of an outsider.

I step into the kitchen and rummage through drawers until I grab a notepad and a pen. Back on the porch swing, I write Dyson a quick note. At first, I stare at the paper, blank like I feel inside. Then the words pour out of me: *How could you do this? I've never felt for anyone the way I feel for you. I let my guard down and you reminded me why I need it in the first place. I thought you cared for me. I thought I loved you.*

Tears dampen the paper as I let loose the flood I've dammed, until I've written all I can, and I have to get out of here. My legs carry me away from the house, the street, the neighborhood, propelled by my broken heart. *How could he do this to me?*

"Illusions," Dad's voice taunts.

"Appearances," Mom's voice echoes.

I'd fallen for him, for this perfect person that he made me believe he was, when all the while he only pretended because he had to, because the Universe had paired us up and given us this gift—this curse—to speak to one another inside our heads. That's all I am to him, a voice he can't shake free. A freak that's trapped to him like a conjoined twin. His nemesis. My legs burn as I sprint to the sanctuary of the familiar woods where I can be alone. All the while I wish I weren't.

I want to hear his voice again, to see his face, to kiss his lips.

And hate myself for it.

Worst of all, I have no way to even tell him that I hate him

That I love him.

I left the note tucked away in one shoe on Lucas's front porch. I still believe he's my Prince Charming.

11

Even if that means I have to stage it to be his Cinderella.

◻◻ CHANNELS ◻◻

Someone pounds on my front door and I wake up Pillow over my head, positive it's Shai, I scream, "Go away!" even though she can't possibly hear and I'll eventually have to get up. After last night, I don't want to deal with anybody, but the knock continues, so I hobble downstairs and open the door. But it isn't Shai. It's her mother.

"Hey, Ms. Dwenger."

"Is Shai here?"

"No. She isn't with you?" It's only now that I see her eyes are puffy from crying. "Do you want to come in?"

She charges past. I close the door and follow her to the kitchen where I lean against the counter as she stares at me, arms crossed.

"What?" I ask.

So, it's a stupid thing to say.

"Where'd you and Shai really go last night?"

With a shrug, I say, "To the movies, like we said," careful not to look Ms. Dwenger in the eyes.

"I'm gonna ask you again, Mahlorie, because I know you are not the type of girl who lies. Where did you and Shai go last night?"

I look up. "To a friend's house. We watched a movie."

"Why are you here without her?"

"It's complicated."

"Spare me. Did Shai stay the night at her boyfriend's house and you're covering?"

"Honestly, I don't know. I mean it. I was having a bad time, so I left and came here. I know I'm not supposed to be here alone, but I didn't want to get Shai in trouble, and I felt like being at home, in my own bed."

"So where was the party?"

"At Lucas—"

Ms. Dwenger's phone rings. "Shai?" she says into the receiver. It's a one-sided conversation, and I hear: "This is she..." followed by a long silence and then, "Are you sure? Which hospital?"

She hangs up and looks at me. "Shai's at the hospital."

"What? Why?"

"She was in a car accident. Drunk driver ran them into a tree. They don't know if..." She starts to cry.

I'm in shock and tell her, "I'm getting dressed, then we're gone."

She nods, and I run upstairs, my mind a mélange of guilt. I left Shai without a word, then didn't answer her calls. And Dyson who stood me up is the catalyst for my wild run home. If I'd only stayed, I never would have let her get in that car. Dressed, I rush back downstairs to a quiet that buzzes in my ears. Shai's mom stopped crying, cheeks flushed, eyes puffy and red.

"Ms. Dwenger?" She looks up. "You okay to drive?"

She nods, and we bolt to her Beemer. The drive to the hospital is the longest of my life. I don't cry, my eyes trained on the bright world outside my window. Without intention, I've turned off my feelings. I've lost contact with Dyson. I can't lose it with Shai, too. They might be the only two people I've ever loved.

□□□□□

We pull into the hospital. Fluorescent lights. Powerful disinfectants. Elevators that take too long to arrive then zip to the floor too quickly. Shai was brought in as a trauma and ushered to ICU. By the time we arrive, they've moved her to a private room in the pediatric wing.

With each open door we pass, my gaze wanders. Broken bones. Pneumonia. Surgery recovery. My palms sweat as I feel the weight of my own mortality. We reach Shai's room, and I'm not prepared for what I see. Her face is cut with ugly purple and yellow bruises along her cheeks. One of her arms hides in a cast. The other attaches to an IV bag. Machines beep her vitals and my feet freeze at the threshold.

Shai's mom barrels past, bursts into tears. She cries out Shai's name over and over again while chills run down my spine. I'm a bystander in a play, only that isn't stage makeup, and this isn't a set.

My insides press against my skin. A sour taste fills my mouth. I'm hot. I'm cold. I've got to get out of here. I zip to the window at the end of the hall, my breath uneven. Outside, the river spills over the horizon, framed by the shores of the mainland to the west and the barrier island to the east. Mansions dot riverfront properties with docks that lead out to boats

11

so large I can make out their dimensions from the fourteenth floor—which is actually the thirteenth, but for superstition and all, that floor doesn't exist.

"It's been three years, George," a woman says from one of the rooms.

I hate to eavesdrop, but their voices carry as the man replies, "He's been in this condition long enough, Patricia. He's gone."

"You don't know that," she says, her voice a tremor of defeat. "People wake up from comas."

I imagine this is a conversation the couple has had many times before. A seagull soars across the sky, and I suddenly picture Dyson's stormy gray eyes. I break down, desperate to hear his voice. "Dyson," I mutter.

"He's gone," says the man in the room. Goosebumps raise the hair on the back of my neck. Is he in my head too? "We have to let him go," the man continues.

The woman's soft sobs filter from the room as someone taps my shoulder. I whip around and face a nurse with mocha skin, her dark hair cropped short around her head. "You okay, miss?"

I nod, wipe my face dry.

"Can I help you?"

"I'm here to visit a friend. Shai Dwenger."

"She's awake now. You can talk to her."

As we pass the room with the man and woman inside, I glance over at a pulled curtain. My lips pull taut. Life is fragile. I lost Dyson and I nearly lost Shai. As I reach the door, I promise myself I won't let her see my fear. I'll be strong, like she always is for me. I walk inside and smile sadly. "Hey, sweetie." I force down bile.

Shai's left eye is bloodshot and cloudy. The

bruise on her face is somehow worse. "Hey," she croaks.

Her neck is wrapped in a brace and I pray it isn't broken, though I'm too afraid to ask. I slide onto the foot of her bed. We're quiet. "Does it hurt?"

"As bad as it looks."

"I doubt that," I joke.

She smirks, then grimaces.

"Sorry," I say. "Stupid joke." What an idiot I can be. "Do you remember what happened?"

"Not really. Jake was driving. He'd been drinking, a lot. We all had." She looks up. "You were right, Mal. They were—"

"Ssshhhh." I slide closer. "It's not important anymore. You're okay. That's all that matters."

A doctor raps on the door, and I stand as he enters the room. "Hello, Miss Dwenger. How are you feeling?" He checks her vitals, adjusts some machines, and faces Shai. "You're one lucky girl. Those boys you came in with, the driver died upon impact with a blood alcohol level of 0.24. That's three times the legal limit.

"The other boy wasn't wearing his seatbelt. He was thrown through the windshield and sustained internal injuries. We were hopeful, but he didn't make it either."

Shai stares blankly ahead. My knees quake, unable to support my weight.

"I'm only telling you this, Miss Dwenger, because I want you to understand the gravity of your situation. One poor decision cost two boys their lives and almost cost you yours. I'm very sorry, but I hope you'll learn from this and their deaths won't be in vain." His face grim, the doctor nods at me, to acknowledge I heard every word too, and then exits the room.

Shai's mom moves from the corner to her daughter's side. Through the pain of a broken face and a broken heart, Shai cries into her mother's chest.

I wish my mother were here.

I wish I was home in my room.

I wish Dyson would say something. "Dyson?" I whisper into cupped hands. Nothing.

I wish Dyson didn't exist.

▫ BLURRED LINE ▫

Back at school, I'm once again the center of attention as everyone asks about Shai.

"What happened?"

"Is she gonna be okay?"

"I heard the car flipped a hundred times."

"I heard those guys she rode with were unrecognizable."

I'm truly disgusted. This isn't about Shai. These aren't people who know her or care about her at all. It's their need to be heard, to be connected to the attention, the glamour of death and destruction. Shai happens to have flirted with the Grim Reaper.

Shai and I talk on the phone some, but mostly we text. She hasn't had much to say since the accident. A piece broke inside her. I don't know what to do to help her, and it kills me. Her mom says to give her time and suggests I talk to a school counselor about it. Not interested. I think I'd rather talk to Dr. Ant Killer, to tell you the truth. There's this new edge to her voice I can't quite discern. Like a piece of her wonders why I left her daughter with those jerks to begin with. Like she blames me for the accident. It bugs me.

Because I know she's right, even if she never says it out loud.

For now, I have to somehow make it through Algebra without Dyson to feed me the answers. Speaking of Dyson, I have more digging to do. Questions to answer. Strings to untangle. I'm not ready to give up yet. My best idea is to hole up in the girl's bathroom, which thankfully, Mrs. Lichtim allows with a hall pass. But my legs carry me past the ladies' room, down the empty hall, toward the media center, where I sit in front of an available computer and enter my student ID. I stare at the blank screen. What am I doing? My fingers push through my hair. My mind wanders the room. This is hopeless. He's gone. I need to accept it. For all I know, he figured out a way to disconnect and he's the one who turned me off.

But I know that's a lie.

His voice still echoes in my memories: "The Universe wanted us to meet."

But why? And if that's true, why did it tear us apart? Life was fine before he came along. Now, it'll never be the same again. I know I have to carry on with the search until I figure it out. Until I hear him again. I come up empty on how. What would Sam and Dean do? You know, the gorgeous heroes from *Supernatural*. They always face crap like this on the show. Dig through the internet. Somehow, their world wide web of weirdness isn't available to the rest of us.

"Mahlorie?"

I turn and the world fills in around me like a curtain rise on Broadway. It's Lucas. He's visibly upset. "Hey," I say. "What's up?"

"You talk to Shai?" He sidles into the seat beside me. He smells of cologne and mint toothpaste. "She won't take my calls or return my texts. I'm going crazy. I never should've let her leave." He shakes his head. "I'll never drink again."

I let him vent his frustration until he's exhausted. Lips quiver, tears threaten to burst, he rubs his palms together as if to wipe them clean of what he believes to be his fault.

"It was an accident, Lucas. You can't blame yourself."

"Can't I?" he says, his eyes sad. "I let her go."

"She went because she wanted to go. You and I both know that when Shai makes up her mind, it'll take an act of Congress to change it. And that might not even work."

He laughs. Wipes his eyes. "She okay?" I shrug. "She will be."

"Will you tell her to call me?"

"Sure."

But we know she won't until she's ready. "Thanks, Mal. See you around."

"See ya," I say as he walks out the glass doors without so much as a glance over his shoulder.

It's funny, but he's perfect for Shai. He brings out a side of her I've never seen before. It's ironic since she only started dating him to be featured in his ESPN reel, for when he made it big and they went back to his humble beginnings. I don't think she'll be in it now. I don't think you can ever go back to "normal" after a life or death experience like she's had. I mean, she loves attention, but not this kind. It's more like a bad rumor that you can't shake. No, it's worse than that. Because of the article in the paper about her accident, it's more like a permanent ding in her public record.

That's when it hits me. Dyson.

His accident. Three years prior. In this county.

I bet my life it's in some newspaper somewhere.

And if it is, I can almost guarantee the reporter listed his last name. Maybe even his address.

The bell rings and I jump out of my seat with the realization that tomorrow I'll be in huge trouble with Mrs. Lichtim because I used her hall pass to skip the entire period. But I don't care. For the first time since we lost communication, I'm hopeful I can find Dyson and confront him face-to-face.

If only to tell him I never want to speak to him again.

▫▫ REVELATIONS ▫▫

If this day could've dragged any slower, it would've turned into yesterday. The final bell rings and I text Dad that I plan to stay after to research in the library. He sends me back a GIF of a mule kicking over a pile of books. I assume that means yes.

The catwalk leads to the media center filled with students who hurry off campus, with chatter about weekend plans. Sometimes, I feel like I'm in the wrong time, like I'm really from the 1800s, an Old West rebel who robbed banks and flirted with disaster. It's probably the genes of Victoria M. Reddish dying to get out and onto the page. Maybe a distant memory of a past life, though I don't really believe in all that. I don't feel like I belong here. I don't fit. And more, I don't wanna fit.

Heavy clouds roll in to warn of afternoon storms. They saturate the air with humid gusts that whip my short hair. Thunder rumbles in hunger as it searches for those in the open to devour, the way it hunted me in the woods near Dyson's cabin. I wish I could go back there, but without his lead, I've no idea where to go. I'd end up an alligator's dinner or permanently lost in the woods.

The media center blasts me with icy air. There's

no one here except the librarian behind the desk checking in books. She peers up, smiles, and focuses back on her task. I enter the computer lab and get online. Where to begin? I wish I could Google "What to Google" and get the answer I need. But it won't be that simple.

I type in "auto accident Brevard County Dyson." A list longer than the Book of Life scrolls across the screen. Too broad. There's even a link to a tragic, in- home accident that involved a Dyson vacuum cleaner. I click on it out of curiosity and immediately wish I hadn't. That image will be burned in my brain for a very long time. I narrow my search field to "teenager car crash three years ago." Another list too long to digest scrolls across, followed by more and more articles. Many list obituaries and I cringe. I ignore every picture possible.

Thunder rumbles as lightning flashes through the large rectangular windows spread nearly floor to ceiling in the sitting area. The wind has really picked up and carries countless pieces of debris in its grasp. Leaves and twigs whip by. Trees bend to touch their toes. I hang my head. What in the world am I doing searching for this boy who probably couldn't care less about me?

Dad texts: **Bad Storm Be there in 5**

So much for research.

Truthfully, I don't believe for a second that Dyson doesn't really care about me. What I wonder about, and what keeps me up at night, is my fear that he's not trying to contact me. I mean, if he really wanted to find me, he could always do a search from Lucas's address, learn his last name, see what school he goes to, then search for Mahlorie in the student records. Okay, I know that's slim, and I know it's not much to go on, but it's more than I have. I know two things: there's a cabin hidden in the woods somewhere that his parents own, and he lives somewhere near Shai's neighborhood—

He knows where Shai lives.

How many 'Shai's' live in her neighborhood? Mahlorie, don't be so dumb. There're hundreds of homes in her development, and it's doubtful that the name of the daughter is listed on each deed. What's he supposed to do, go door to door like a vacuum salesman? I smirk at my corny joke. Tap my fingernails on the keys.

What else do I know?

Only that he has the most beautiful eyes I've ever seen, and he writes amazing poetry and…

Thunder cracks, closer this time, like the sound when lightning struck me. When my metal mouth somehow connected with the plate in Dyson's head.

That's it.

Rain slams the tin roof, lightning blasts, and thunder hammers as the storm reaches us. Suddenly, the power goes out.

Dad texts: **Outside**

In frustration, I grab my bag and run out to Dad's car. I'm drenched by the time I close the door and silence the storm.

"Hey, turtledove," Dad says. "Barely missed the storm.

The story of my life. We drive home.

My mind whirls as I consider how close I am to actually find him. I mean, how many kids named Dyson were in a car crash three years ago that left a metal plate in their heads? Even though the something that brought us together has also silenced us, Pandora's Box is within my grasp.

But opening Pandora's Box always leads to trouble.

▫▫ STATIC ▫▫

After a hot shower, I'm warmed up and sit cross- legged on my blanket in comfy pants. Wet strands of hair that aren't quite long enough to catch behind my ears fall in my face as I open my laptop to continue my search.

"Okay, Dyson. Where are you?"

I type in "Brevard County car accident teenager metal plate" hopeful that I've picked the right keyword combination to unlock the information I so desperately need. And with a nearly audible pop, the list flashes before my eyes. I open several links, amazed to discover the sheer number of teenagers that underwent automobile accidents in my county that resulted in metal plates screwed into their skulls. Unfortunately for me, none of them list names or addresses, since the Privacy Act prevents the newspapers from listing this information without parental consent.

Perfect. The one time I need to know, I can't access the details. Useless. Now what? This is so unfair. All of it. I didn't ask to meet him. I wasn't looking for an incredible guy to fall in love with. He came to me. He was brought to me. For what? To have him ripped away, never to be found again?

I wish I could talk to Shai about this. I'd tell her the whole story, every single little detail, even if she has no bright ideas to help. It'd be nice to have someone to wallow in self-pity with. I want Shai by my side. But what am I thinking? She's been through a trauma, and all I care about are my stupid problems, which really aren't problems at all.

Dyson's gone. Period.

And I won't let him go.

The storm continues in flashes outside my blinds with thunder too close behind. I lean back against my headboard. A tear slides down my cheek, drips off my chin. I close my laptop and move it to the side table next to the small box that holds my broken brace and the wrinkled picture I drew from memory of Dyson's face. All it needs is a candle and it'll be a shrine.

Ridiculous.

I take the box. Open it. Observe the small piece of metal between my fingers. Turn it around as if I'll learn a new truth from another angle, like it holds the answers to my problems within its very fibers. I close my eyes.

I drift.

Sounds appear, fuzzy, as fuzzy snow. Rain streaks in stretched lines. Static from the old television in my great-grandmother's basement, where I have to hold the antennae to get the picture to stabilize.

Then a voice.

Broken. Pierced and splotched. A crackled CB in an old trucker movie I remember watching as a kid, probably in that very same basement. When the driver is out of range.

"...llo...you...al..ee..."

A dream.

It must be because I swear it's Dyson. Muffled. Distant. My hand closes tighter on the stupid brace and I roll onto my side, fist to my cheek.

It's clearer.

"ello...there...Mahl..."

This is a wonderful dream. I won't ever wake up. In my half-sleep, half-awake state, I answer, "Hello, Dyson. Long time no see. How've you been?"

I smile.

"...al," I hear back, *"...you...ear...me..."*

"What?" I mind whisper in a euphoric state. "What Dyson? I can't hear you. Speak louder."

A chill rakes my spine and my eyes pop open as a bolt of lightning cracks right outside my window. At the same moment, as if he lies in bed beside me, I can hear Dyson loud and clear shout, *"MAHLORIE!"*

And as Frankenstein reanimated into Mary Shelley's monster, so too, my heart pumps to life as I understand that somehow, Dyson has returned.

▫▫ DIRECTION ▫▫

"Dyson? You there?"

Silence.

"No, no, no…not again." I leap from my bed, pace the floor. I can't handle this anymore!

"Mahlorie? You hear me?"

I'm not sure how I hadn't noticed it before, but it occurs to me why I can suddenly hear Dyson again. As my fingers brush my dark locks, the metal brace in my hand moves closer to my ear closer to my metal mouth.

I test my theory and touch the bracket to my braces. Dyson's voice rings clear.

"Is it really you?" he asks.

Part of me finds the question silly, as I wonder how many other girls he might communicate with in his head. "Yes," I say, my thumb keeps the bracket in place. "I can't believe you're back."

"I never thought I'd hear your voice again."

"Me neither." Warmth fills me as I forget every frustration and angry thought I've had, wanting only to talk with him forever. Never wanting to be without him again. "I've been looking all over for you."

Lightning flashes in quick successions, which strengthen his voice as it boosts our connection. *"Me too.*"

"Have you?" The sudden coldness to my voice is out of my control. I guess I am still ticked off after all.

"Of course, Mal. I've been going crazy looking for you. Once you dropped off, I... well, it hasn't been the same."

"Then why'd you stand me up?"

"It's not like that."

Heat rises. "That's sure what it looks like to me. You know I left you a note. In my shoe. In case you actually came. God. I'm so stupid. This is why falling in love sucks."

"I didn't have a ride."

"What?"

"A ride. I couldn't get there."

"So, you left me hanging. Do you know how much that hurt? I walked all the way to your cabin, and you couldn't meet me then either. What, is this too inconvenient for you? Am I not worth it?"

"I'm wheelchair bound, okay?"

Silence.

Air sucked from the room silence.

"You're...I don't understand."

"The crash. My spine severed, and I can't walk. I'm in a wheelchair, so I couldn't wheel all the way there and back. I don't expect you to understand. I'm so sorry, Mal. I never meant to hurt you."

"Why didn't you tell me?"

He sneers. *"I couldn't."*

"Why not?"

"What if it changed things? What if you found out I was crippled, and you never wanted to talk to me again? Which really sucks for you if I'm stuck in your head. That's why I told you not to go looking for

13

me if the connection ever broke. I figured we'd get as much time as whatever brought us together allowed and that was it. I never really thought we'd meet in person. Most of the time I think I made you up, you know, like you're this voice inside my head that I created to cope. I wonder if you're even real half the time."

"Well, I am. And you should have told me."

"Maybe. Does it change anything?"

"No, nothing at all," I say, though my voice pinches and I wonder, does it change anything? It shouldn't, right? He's the same incredible guy I fell in love with. But then I imagine Shai's expression when I tell her that my boyfriend is a cripple who rides around in a wheelchair. And that thought angers me. Not because of how I know Shai would react, but because if I'm being honest, I think it would bother me.

"Appearance is everything," Mom whispers in my mind.

No, Victoria. You're wrong. Appearance is meaningless. I love this boy, and I don't care what anyone says.

"It doesn't change a thing, Dyson. I don't care about that."

"Really?" Huge sigh. *"That's a relief. You sure? I mean, you're not mad at me anymore?"*

"I thought you'd stood me up."

"Are you kidding me? Never. Not in a million years would I miss a chance to be with you."

I swallow hard. "Me neither." My thoughts drift to that night, to the emptiness inside, then to Shai and how I'd abandoned her to those creeps, how she'd nearly been killed.

My voice must falter because Dyson asks,

"What's wrong? Don't believe me?"

"No, it's not that. I believe you. It's…Shai got hurt that night. She got in a bad car crash with these two idiots and she could've died. I wasn't with her, but she got in with a drunk driver, and…well, he died. It scared me so much and I needed you, and you weren't there anymore."

"I'm so sorry, Mal. Is she okay?"

"She will be."

"Are you okay?"

"I am now."

The storm draws near, and rain falls in fat drops. Each lightning bolt strengthens our reception to the point where static crackles in my teeth.

"Do you know what happened with us?" Dyson asks. *"Why we lost communication? And more importantly, how we got it back?"*

"I think so. It's my braces. A bracket popped out at Dr. Ant Killer's—that's what I call my dentist— and I knew you were gone as soon as it happened."

"Wait, wait. Hold up. You call your dentist 'Dr. Ant Killer'?"

"Not to his face. You know, he's like that type of person who as a kid used a magnifying glass to fry ants. I mean, who else would grow up and become an orthodontist? On purpose?"

Dyson laughs. God, I've missed his laugh.

"How'd you get us back?"

"The bracket. I grabbed it off the floor in case. I'm literally holding it against my braces right now. I think the lightning somehow makes the frequency stronger."

"Sure, it is. Spherics."

"Huh?"

"It's the radio waves discharged when

13

lightning strikes. Like when you're listening to the AM station in the car and static shoots out and muffles it really quick. That's the spherics from the spark plug discharges in the engine."

"Man, homeschoolers sure do learn weird stuff."

"You have no idea."

Before he's gone, and I can't hear his voice anymore, I say, "I can't lose you again." Thunder stampedes overhead, my voice a whisper. "I can't."

"You won't. I promise."

But his promises are empty and we both know it. I don't know why we can hear each other, but the forces that brought us together can easily rip us apart. We know this. We've been through it once already.

"How?" I ask. "How will you promise?"

His silence cracks as the diminished clouds whisk the storm over and past my house. It'll be over soon. The storm, the signal. He'll be gone again, a scent caught in my hair.

"I don't really know much about you," he says. *"That would help."* His voice fades. The storm pulls him away.

Why did I waste so much time? He's right. We know next to nothing about each other. That's why it was so difficult to search for him. "What's your last name?" I ask. "Where do you live?"

"Hon...st...es...Mal?" he says. *"Can...ear...e..."*

"NO! Not yet. Dyson, what's your last name?"

"Wh...Ma...ame..."

"What's. Your. Last. Name?" My words stretch like taffy.

"He...s."

"What?" I screech in desperation as my fingers twist the brace for better purchase.

"He...ts."

"Hets? Dyson Hets?" I beg.

"Hertz!"

And I almost laugh, though my heart breaks as he dies with the storm.

Hertz.

The boy in my head who speaks to me through a shared frequency is called Hertz.

▫▫ THE WEB ▫▫

My fingers tap the keyboard tentatively, as if I'm about to uncover a long-lost secret, like who really shot JFK or whether aliens built the pyramids. I type *Dyson Hertz Melbourne Florida* into the search bar and hold my breath.

Both keywords highlight in unrelated links for local cleaning services, vacuum companies, and electrical websites. I scroll down a few pages and see a Facebook link for one of the cleaning companies. I click through to do an internal search on the site for Dyson Hertz. Only one profile pops up. My heart hammers as I click on it.

Those eyes. Those lips.

I've found him.

I read the description and notice the last post was more than three years ago. What does that mean? I click on friend request and don't learn much more than I already know, since his education lists 'homeschooled' and his address is unlisted. I'm able to access a small group of his pics and friends, but none are common, and the pics are outdated by several years.

I'm totally thrown. The whole site reeks of

three years ago. I wonder why he hasn't posted. Why the page is even still active? Especially since now I know that he's in a wheelchair and probably doesn't leave his home too much. God, where did that come from? Like because he sits in a chair means he's homebound. That's so stupid, but why is it the first thing that pops in my head?

Because it matters, a still voice in my head whispers.

Because you're a fraud who really does care about what he looks like.

"No!" I scream out. "It's not true. I love him, and I don't believe that for a second." I scold myself until I actually believe what I preach. Imagine I bring him home—my mom's face, my dad's questions—and in this vision, Dyson doesn't skip a beat, as he answers Dad's onslaught about how we met and "his intentions with his daughter" and my mother's barrage about what it's like to be unable to walk as she plans a character in her next book.

I would be proud to stand by his side.

I wonder if he'd let me sit on his lap and we could race down the road. I smirk at the thought as I search for him on a few other social media sites to end my hunt right back where I started.

Empty.

How can this guy have no online presence? And why in the world didn't we exchange phone numbers? I'm not ready to give up though and spend the next few hours searching until my crossed eyes scream for a reprieve. And before I give up, I find a totally random page that almost pops up on its own, which lists George and Patricia Hertz ages 49-52 and Dyson Hertz associated with the couple, all at an unlisted address in Melbourne, Florida. For $44.99, I can access the address.

My parents have a credit card in the kitchen drawer for emergencies. This is definitely an emergency. I creep downstairs to grab the card and run, but Dad slices vegetables for dinner.

"Hey, turtledove. How's it going?"

"Fine."

"You hungry?"

"I guess."

"Good. Cause I'm starved. Wanna help?"

"Not really." I open the drawer and slip my hand inside, feeling around for the plastic card.

"That's fine. Anything new in school? Any word on Shai? A boyfriend?"

My face is ice as the color drains. "Boyfriend?" The knife stops.

My hand retreats. Drawer closes.

Dad faces me. "Something you're not telling? I was simply fishing for small talk. Is there a boyfriend these days I need to worry about?"

I smile my cutest *you're-the-only-man-for-me- daddy* while I shake my head. Dad's eyes narrow. He stares hard at my mouth.

"What is that?" He points at the bracket.

My lips are a magician's sheet that hide my braces from Dad's inspection. With a flick of the tongue, I work the bracket free and slip it between my cheek and gum. Ta-Da! Sleight of hand...or tongue in cheek, in my case.

"What is what?" I ask, sweetly.

"Smile again," he said.

I comply, blink dramatically to ease his concerns. "Everything okay?" I ask.

But it's written across his face. Dad knows better. His instincts warn him that a trick's been played and he's the butt of the joke. "Your brace was twisted. Now it's not." He returns to the vegetables and I continue to rummage through the drawer, both the criminal and lookout all at once. "Your mother and I work hard to pay for your teeth to be straightened. And it isn't cheap. Believe me. So, I don't find it very funny when you screw with your braces then pretend like—"

"I didn't screw with them."

"I saw it with my own eyes, Mahlorie. Something was stuck to your braces then you moved it. Don't think for a second, I don't see things as they are. It's my job to convince people what they see is real, while I'm pulling one over on them. Know how it works, inside and out, sweetheart. You did something and now you're trying to convince both of us you didn't."

"But Dad—"

Knife down.

Shoulders clenched.

Lines crossed.

I quickly close the drawer again, no card.

"Mahlorie, I've had enough. You had a chance to explain yourself, an opportunity to come clean. You chose to lie. Now, you and your tricky tongue can spend the rest of the night up in your room. How about that?"

With a huff, I stomp out of the kitchen, up the stairs, without the credit card, and suddenly in trouble. How did this happen? I'm halfway up when Dad screams, "And no electronics."

To this, I let out an audible grunt of frustration. Back in my room, I close the door and flop onto my bed. The loose bracket goes back in the box along with any hope of finding Dyson. I move to close my laptop, when an idea strikes me.

I know I'm not supposed to, but I open Google and type *George and Patricia Hertz Melbourne Florida Cabin.* Seconds pass wrapped in forever when a map flashes onto the screen. It's an aerial of the cabin with two addresses listed beneath it. One seems to belong to the cabin itself. The other, I bet my life, is to Dyson's house.

⸬OUT OF ORDER⸬

The night drags and I flit in and out of dreams, where Dyson's in my head, then by my side, then yanked back into silent darkness out of my grasp. Tears seep from my closed eyes, the vivid dreams simply mirror my fragmented reality.

It's Saturday and my big plans are to head straight into the lion's den. Yup, I'm biking to the address off the internet to knock on Dyson's front door. Of course, I know how dangerous it is. And stupid. And improbable that it's even his house. But with the weatherman predicting fair skies all weekend, I'm out of excuses. I pocket the faulty bracket.

Dad works in the loft on a new trick, so he's more than happy to let me go "to the library" so he'll have a quiet house to himself. I grab the credit card from the kitchen for any unexpected emergencies, pack a lunch, and head out. The sun warms my back. Wind whips past my ears. I take the streets to the edge of my neighborhood, then back roads as often as possible, and only enter major highways as I near his street. My heart races. Adrenaline chokes me.

What am I doing? I am undeniably the stupidest person on the planet. Who uses information off the internet to guide them to a stranger's front door? But my pace doesn't slow, as I turn into his neighborhood, a quaint cookie-cutter development with a single way in and out. Branches stretch overhead like nets ready to fall and capture me. Lilacs perfume the air like noxious gas ready to suffocate me. I bet Victoria would appreciate my overactive imagination, after she killed me off for being a moron.

The road curves, straightens, curves again, and a stop sign looms ahead. To the right, a park frames the street beside a basketball court and open field. I bet Dyson loved growing up here. I pass the park, follow the road as it loops to the back, and see his house come in view along the corner. Sick to my stomach, I pass his house. Maybe I'll go home, or better yet, maybe I'll actually go to the library like I told Dad I would.

I can forget him…if I try really hard.

No storms, no static, no four-letter words to haunt me with visions of what could've been, if only.

I could forget…if I went to sleep and never woke up.

I turn my bike around, reach his driveway, and park in the grass. Tentatively, I walk up the paved path to the front walk bordered by fragrant flower bushes and small manicured shrubs. A handicap ramp leads to an oversized door. This must be it. I peer in through the frosted glass panes, unable to clearly define what's inside. And with my heart about to burst through my chest, I ring the doorbell. The hollow gong resonates off high ceilings to alert the owners of my presence.

Can't turn back now.

Movement blurs through the panes as an underwater wave rolls toward shore.

Locks click. Knob turns. Door opens.

The woman who stands before me appears much older than the information from Google suggested.

Gray hair curls brush her shoulders. Sharp eyes peer upon me with curiosity. "May I help you?" she asks curtly.

I swallow my voice, clear my throat, and say, "I'm looking for someone."

A half-smile curves her mouth, "Well, who, dear?" I look past her at the perfectly ordered home.

How does a teenaged boy fit in?

A man wheels up in a chair alongside her. "Who is it?" he asks, but when he sees me, his face lights up. "Is it cookie time already?"

My brow crinkles, then I understand his mistaken assumption. "No, sir. I'm not a Girl Scout. I'm looking for someone." Why don't I say his name? What's the matter with me?

"Oh?" The man nudges the woman out of his way and opens the door wider. "Who is it that you're looking for, honey?"

"A boy."

Their faces don't change. Mine does. "About my age."

Nothing registers.

"The information I got off the internet said this was his address."

"You're out knocking on strangers' front doors lookin' for a boy that the interweb said lives here?"

The man is livid. "Don't you know how dangerous that is? 'Specially for a young girl like you who's probably never been in trouble a day in her life."

He doesn't know me. "Yes, sir. I understand—"

"No, you don't. You wouldn't be knocking on my door looking for a boy. Who is this boy anyway? You know him? Or did ya meet him on the interweb too?"

My voice shakes. "So you don't have a son." I take a step back. My heart is broken.

"No, dear," the woman adds. "Not near your age, at any rate."

The man faces the woman. "Didn't that couple we bought the house from have a son? He'd be about the girl's age by now, wouldn't he? Maybe a tinge older? Had a funny name, too? Mayson...Greyson..."

"Dyson?" I manage.

"Yes," the woman says. "That sounds about right. Is that the boy you're looking for, dear?"

I nod. "Do you know where they moved to? I really need to get in touch with him. I'm not a stalker or anything weird like that. I...lost his number and have been trying to reach him for a while now. I'm kind of desperate at this point."

The couple exchanges a glance. Maybe I said too much.

"I'm afraid not, dear," the woman says.

"Would a been four years ago, this May," the man adds. "Probably not even in the same place even if we did have a forwarding' address."

"Now why would you say that?" the woman asks. "We still live in the same place."

"But we're retired, Beth. This'll be the last place either of us call home, lessen God takes me first, in which case you'll probably sell the thing off and live on a cruise ship the rest of your days."

The woman smiles, then turns to me. "I'm sorry we couldn't be of help, dear. But promise me you won't go knocking on stranger's doors anymore."

"I promise," I lie. That's exactly what I plan to do.

"That's right, young lady. You got lucky meeting us. We're two old geezers who wouldn't hurt a fly."

"Speak for yourself," the woman adds, "at least about the old part."

Salutations.

Door closes.

Silence.

I want to ring the bell again, pry further. Look through their attic for the box that contains any paperwork from when they purchased the house four years ago. There has to be a forwarding address with the post office, for at least the first year. Would they still have that? Does that information disappear? Can they legally release it to anyone?

Maybe they would let me walk through the house, go into his old bedroom, and look in a secret place for a letter he'd left me before we even met. A supernatural sign that could bring us together again.

But I do none of that.

I walk back to my bike, as my phone vibrates. It's a text from Shai's mom:

Hospital. Now.

Those two words send me into a tailspin and, in a haze, I'm back on my bike, pedaling with all my strength to the hospital less than a mile away. My thighs are on fire. Lungs burn as I maneuver away from his house, his neighborhood, back on the main highway. Farther and farther from Dyson with every second. I'm near exhaustion when I reach the hospital entrance, text for the room number, and ride the elevator back to the pediatric wing.

Shock shrouds me as I stare at my best friend

attached to wires with a tube down her throat, in a hospital bed, unconscious. Her mother wraps her arms around me and whispers that Shai has slipped into a coma.

▫▫ LOST ▫▫

It's called *subdural hematoma*.

Small veins bleed slowly, collect in the skull, and compress the brain. Shai's type is chronic, which means she's bled for weeks, since the accident, but no one's noticed any symptoms. I thought she was depressed, even traumatized by the accident and death of the twins. Maybe Survivor's Remorse. But never bleeding. Never a concussion. Never physical. It's like when a hose leaks, slow and steady, unnoticed…until you get the water bill. Then you know something's wrong. That's what's happened to Shai. The clotted blood triggered her body to power down, but not shut off. She lies in a coma, with her mother and I helplessly alone.

I stay with her mom until she's calm and I'm numb. It's my typical response to real life problems: feel nothing. If I don't feel, I can't hurt. But this pain is so great, even my self-preservation fails me. Why don't our bodies respond to emotional pain the same way as physical pain? If my heart is breaking, why doesn't my brain notice and drop me into an emotional coma?

It's not fair.

My dad arrives and leads me to the car, my bike tossed in the back. He doesn't say a word and I'm grateful. This isn't his comfort zone either. Real life seems to scare the magic right out of him. There's no sleight of hand that can change this. A make-believe chant holds no power over Shai's fate. She is at the mercy of the unseen—the man behind the curtain.

Control is the illusion we buy into.

People will believe what they want to be real. *That's* the only truth. My dad doesn't control the audience. They choose to suspend their disbelief, so they can enjoy the tricks. Dad is wrong. And Mom's whole career is based on this concept. She writes lies and calls it fiction, then lives those lies by portraying her brand in the public eye. But underneath all that wardrobe, hair, and make-up, she's like everyone else: powerless. Appearance isn't everything. Mom is wrong too.

I spend the weekend in my room silent, barely eating, and, for some reason, writing. Most of it is angry and frustrated. The rest are apology letters to Shai for abandonment and unshared secrets and the pain that I allowed to touch our lives. My tears soak through the pages, smudge the penciled words she may never read.

Her mom texts periodically. No change.

No response.

I don't reply beyond, "Okay." I can't.

My other letters are written to Dyson. Those take longer to write and don't say as much. What can I write? The most I can scribble is "Where are you?" before I cry all over again. Why did this happen to me?

Whose idea was it to rip away the only two people who matter to me? At least if Dyson was still in my head, I could make it through. But I don't know where he is. And honestly, I'm over it.

My bones are tired. My heart is numb. My brain aches.

By Sunday evening, my parents are both gone, Dad on a ship in the Caribbean and Mom to a book signing in Toronto. They apologetically explain how they wish they could stay but can't. I ignore them. They could reschedule. They could stay. But they'd rather flee, get as far away from this as possible. Jump back into their illusions powered by the applause from their fans, and I'm angry. Not because they're gone, but because they get to escape.

I jump in the shower, hoping the water will cleanse my body and soul. Exhausted, an idea begins to form, like a spark fans a flame into a brushfire. I come to a decision. Tonight, after Mrs. Cardillo is passed out—the only babysitter left for my overprotective parents—I plan to sneak out to find Dyson's cabin in the woods, to find him, and I won't stop until we're face to face or I'm dead from trying.

▫▫ RUNAWAY ▫▫

I swear, I never thought Mrs. Cardillo would pass out. The wine didn't flow till almost 8:30—a record for her, in an attempt to show restraint after what happened the last time she watched me, I'm sure—but once she starts, she polishes off two bottles like she's in a race to make up for lost time. By 11:45, she's accomplished her goal. Light snores bounce off her ample chest where her head rests. I almost feel bad, with how irate my parents will be when they find out. But that's what they get when an incompetent guardian watches their daughter, who is way too old to still have a babysitter, by the way, although Mom and Dad would never entertain that conversation.

At least all that guilt means I won't get into as much trouble.

My bag's packed and I'm a little more prepared this time around about what I may face. Snacks, charged cell phone, flashlight, and extra batteries inside a waterproof bag. My magic bracket is wedged in my mouth, clamped to my braces by fishing line and clasps my dad uses to "make things disappear" during his shows. It hurts at first. The nylon scratches my gums and the clamp presses into my cheek, but I barely notice now. Well, except when I look in the mirror, where a mechanical snaggle-toothed walrus stares back at me.

I creep by my passed-out guardian and leave a note on the end table beside her. In the morning, she'll at least be able to tell my parents I'm fine and I'm sorry, but I had to take care of some important business (followed by a few choice words I know I can get away with to let them know exactly how I feel about a wino,—" No, offense, Mrs. C. "—for a babysitter, question their judgment, and basically ensure my punishment-free consequence.)

I think it'll work.

Outside, a cloak of darkness covers me as I ride to the edge of my property and the woods that line my neighborhood. I take a deep breath. I know it's stupid, to blindly trek into the woods alone. I know I only survived the first time around because Dyson guided in my head.

But I have to find him.

I send a text to Shai I know she may never get, tell her I'm sorry for what happened. I never should've left her alone. I explain how I plan to find the boy I told her about. She'll know who I mean. If she ever wakes up. No, when she wakes up. It wouldn't be fair if she stayed this way forever. With tears, I text Shai that I love her and hit send. My heart leaves my chest. The pain is unbearable.

I dump my bike inside the tree line—I don't want to make it too easy for them to find me—and click on the flashlight. The beam assaults the grayscale forest as I step inside the shadows of a labyrinth that I pray will lead me to Dyson.

▫▫ REWIND ▫▫

The clouds block out the moon and stars. My flashlight beam leads me across a dirt path. Night stretches through the crunch of leaves and sticks that snap beneath my feet.

An owl hoots.

Distant thunder rumbles. My heart skips a beat. Really? Again? So much for no storms.

Lightning flashes behind the clouds, angry and full of promise that it will reach me before I reach the cabin. *If* I reach the cabin. Dyson isn't in my head, but he still leads me. He's the reason I press through the evergreen needles that rake against my skin and draw blood. He's the reason I face the darkness, the unknown, the punishment. I have to at least try, or I'll hate myself forever.

Thunder growls as I sprint over the pathway, lurch across fallen trees, and duck beneath low-hanging limbs.

Flash!

Swerve around holes.

Crack!

Leap over rocks.

Boom!

The storm reveals its sheer strength and size

only when the lightning illuminates. It closes in, and I have no way to know how far I am from the cabin or how far I've come from home. Staggered breath comes in gasps. Muscles sear. Sneakers smack against compact dirt. No…there's a blanket of leaves beneath me.

How'd I miss that? How long has it been like this? I stop. Spin. Scan the prism of woods. Where did I stray? When did I leave the path? Lightning races, but thunder gains. I won't make it. I don't know where I am. I can't even go home. I'm lost. Lost in the woods.

"Don't panic, Mal," I speak beneath my breath.

But I don't listen. Panic burns in my chest. I can't escape. I'm gonna lose it. More thunder. More lightning. The flashes are closer now, a flicker of film, and I glance ahead, behind, everywhere, and then I see it. The faint glint, almost a glimmer that I nearly missed.

Water. Reflection. The bridge.

I've never left the path. It'd been covered with leaves and caked mud from other storms. Rush of water greets me, while I carefully teeter across the sandbar—the rotten log border—grateful the rain hasn't flooded the banks yet. Now across and on the path, with brush on both sides, I know I'm closer.

Winds grow into a howl, blow sand in my eyes. I squint against the storm. It will not beat me. A new determination burns a fire inside me. I will make it. I will. I must.

I trudge through the wind and debris and thick darkness. My flashlight beam falls on the oak that nearly killed me when the lightning struck and knocked it over the last time I was in these woods. Only this time, I see a hole dug out by animals to pass through to the other side.

Thank you, God, for small miracles.

I carefully squeeze through the small space. A hiss shifts my heart into overdrive. I jump out the backside, which is too small for me, and break off some of the brittle outer wood. A family of black spiders pours into my hair and down my shirt. I almost pass out. But I force myself to stay in the moment, swat at my face, neck, and arms, shake out my hair, and pull at my shirt. I force my scream to stay within my closed lips. I don't think I could survive if a spider were to crawl inside my mouth.

They still wriggle all over me. I run and leap into the water, and do not surface until I'm convinced the hitchhikers have given up and swam away. I shoot up at the last possible second and break through the surface with a gasp. A quick check of my hair produces no more arachnids.

A splash in the water stops my blood and steals my breath. I don't turn to look because I know what it is. It doesn't sound so close that I can't try to swim toward shore, and I pray I'm right. At the bank, I reach up. Mangroves block my escape. I scoot along, ignore the urge to look back, and grapple for purchase among the unforgiving roots.

This can't be happening.

I peer over my shoulder as lightning reflects off the water that is puddled on the hard plates of the gator's head and back. Its streamlined form zeroes in on me. I jerk around, frantic for a foothold as I push across the bank. Nothing. The storm rolls closer. Thunder rushes. Winds bend trees. Lightning strikes.

Rain sweeps in a rush across the distant trees and grows louder and louder as it approaches. If I don't get out before that rain hits, I'm done for. The mangroves could become too slippery to climb.

The gator growls. How close is it now?

My hands reach beneath the roots to pull myself across and pain shoots through my arms. I hold them up. My hands bleed. The lightning exposes cuts from the mangroves. I can feel my pulse in my palms. Still, I grab ahold and slide across, tears in my eyes, as any second the razor teeth and locked jaws of the monster will reach me.

How did I get here? How did this happen to me?

Never in my life would I be in the woods alone at night. Never. But he is worth it, and whatever brought us together knows this. I dig my feet into the roots, my hands sliced further, as I catch onto something solid, like a shelf in the bank. I'm able to lift up, but not quickly enough. The gator closes in. My eyes shut as I force my muscles to tighten, to push, to lift me out of death's jaws before I'm gator grub.

"Please," I beg. "Help me."

Lightning strikes in simultaneous bolts. I grunt and groan, stretch my muscles. Thunder's right on top of it.

I'm halfway out of the water.

Then, a crack splinters wood in a flash of light, followed by a heavy splash, before the downpour's loosed from the sky. I army crawl out of the water, crying hysterically, and force myself to my feet. Flashlight in hand, I spread the shaky beam across the water.

A limb smokes still ablaze where the lightning struck and broke it off the majestic trunk, juts out of the water between where I hung onto the bank and the gator stalked. The creature's nowhere to be seen. I stumble in a half-run down the right fork toward Dyson's cabin.

I'm so close.

Drenched, shaken, I run toward my last hope.

I'm yards away when light strikes the cabin and catapults me through the air. I smack into a tree, the air knocked out of my lungs. With a gasp, I struggle to focus through the white spots that slowly recede from my vision.

But the glow remains. Burns.

Wood crackles and spits.

Fire consumes the cabin like hungry orange mouths that devour the wood, lick up the walls, melt the frame—the pictures on the mantle and the clothes in the closets and the very bed I slept on when he stayed with me until I fell asleep.

Everything.

Everything that ties him to me. Gone.

Enraged, I rush the cabin, my anger hotter than the fire. I want it to take me, to burn me into ash too. But as I near the tendrils of heat that whip out into black smoke, I fall to my knees.

I am too afraid to move closer. I don't want to die.

I don't want to live.

Rain falls, but not hard enough. Thunder and lightning play their morbid dance, unaware of the damage they cause. My tears cease, replaced with rage. Why? Why is this my fate?

I look up to the power of the storm and scream, "Is this what you want? To destroy me?" My outstretched arms wish to strike, though the unseen cannot be harmed. "Why did you do this to me? I was fine, you hear me? Fine before him! Do you hear me?" Tears stream in a downpour. My broken heart's engulfed in flame. "What was the point...to any of this? What possible—?"

Lightning.

Hair on end. Smells burnt. On my back again.

Am I struck? I thought lightning didn't do that twice.

No, but close.

My ears ring. I can barely move. Water trickles off my fingertips, down my face.

Dyson says my name. I smile. I can see his face.

Those eyes. My lips form his name, breathless. "Dyson."

"Mahlorie, can you hear me?"

My muddled mind slowly clears. Is it really him? I force my head to turn, my torso, till I'm on my stomach.

"Mahlorie, say something."

It *is* him. He's back. And I'm not dead. A million thoughts cross my mind. Did the Universe answer? Was I struck twice? Can he hear me if I talk? Will he leave again? But I simply laugh. Big hard laughter that shakes my battered body until I can't breathe.

Dyson's in my head.

My world is as it should be.

I lie on my stomach as the storm takes the thunder and lightning away, and most likely Dyson, with it. It's almost quiet again. The patter of rain comforts as thunder purrs in the distance.

I sigh. Exhausted. Beat down. Alone.

"Mahlorie?"

He's here. I can still hear him. "Dyson?"

"Oh, my God! Are you okay?"

"I am now," I say, though my broken body says

otherwise.

"Where are you?" he asks.

"That doesn't matter. Tell me where you live. I'm on my way."

PART THREE

The Truth

◻◻ HOME ◻◻

I reach Dyson's neighborhood as morning light paints the sky in orange flames. I'm beyond exhausted, battered, bruised, bloodied, and absolutely ecstatic. He stays in my head all night as a guide dog to the majestic wrought iron gated community he calls home.

Butterflies churn in my stomach the closer I get. I know I look a wreck, but I don't care. There'll be plenty of time to shower and change for our second face-to- face. For this one, I need to see him, tangible, real. One kiss. One gentle stroke of his hand on my cheek. One glance to lock our eyes.

I have to. I will not back down.

Light streams through the trees as I punch in his gate code and the door swings open on silent hinges. I sneak inside on the verge of giggles, like a little girl about to peek at Christmas presents before the house wakes up.

"How long have you lived here?" I ask.

"Only a few years. My parents moved us here before the accident."

"Is that, like, your point of reference? BA-AA. Before accident-after accident?"

His voice smiles. "Yeah. Something like that. A

moment that changes you so much there's a distinction now, between who you were before and who you've become."

"You mean like suddenly hearing a voice in your head?"

"Exactly."

"So, my new point of reference is BD-AD. Before Dyson-after Dyson."

"That sounds way too melodramatic."

"I know it's not as impressive as a plate in your head, but…"

"Is life ever gonna be the same after this?" I don't answer because we both already know. *"It's as if you've saved my life somehow. Like before you, I was surrounded by darkness and then, BAM, everything lit up and I could feel again."*

"I know what you mean. Like something was missing, only you hadn't noticed it before, but now that you've had a taste, you can't go without." I let out a deep breath, my shuffling feet ready to give way.

"You pass the clubhouse yet?" he asks.

"Just did."

"I'm around the bend. I'll meet you out in the yard."

"You know I'm a mess, right?" my nerves make me say.

He laughs. *"I don't care if you're covered in bear crap. I'm grabbing you tight and never letting go."*

I've found him. I really have and I'm so close to seeing him. The journey's been worth it. My feet smack the pavement as I find my second wind and begin to run. But as I round the corner, he's not there. No Dyson in a wheelchair in his yard. My smile fades. Feet stop. "Dyson? Where are you? I said I didn't care

16

about your wheelchair, remember. C'mon. I look like the forest threw up on me and I'm here."

Radio silence.

"Are you messing with me? Cause it's not funny." No answer. Slowly, I approach his drive and head for the front door. No wheelchair ramp? Ecstasy ebbs into confusion. "Why are you doing this?"

Static.

Angry, I reach the threshold and ring the bell. It's probably not even seven, but I don't care. I've had enough. Who does he think he is? If I wasn't exhausted, I might turn around and leave, walk away, and forget all about him for good.

But I'm here. And I won't leave until he faces me. I pound torn hands on the heavy door. Rage eclipses the pain in my heart. I'm about to ring the bell for a second time when the deadbolt turns and the door creaks open. Adrenaline steals my words.

An older woman in a bathrobe with disheveled gray hair stands before me, the sleep not hidden in her voice. "Yes? May I help you?"

It isn't even him. Coward.

"Young lady," the woman says sternly, "is there a reason you're on my doorstep at seven a.m.?"

"Is this the Hertz residence?"

She perks up. "Yes, dear. I'm Mrs. Hertz."

I swallow hard. "I'm sorry to barge in like this. I'm a friend of your son's and he was supposed to meet me here."

She steps back, as a man walks up beside her. "Who is it, Patricia?"

The man has Dyson's same eyes, and I suddenly recognize these people from the pictures on the mantle at the cabin. This *is* his house, and these *are* his parents. Now, I'm pissed. After all we've been through and what I've done to get here, he avoids our face to face?

"I'm Dyson's friend," I say. "I need to speak to him. Could you please ask him to come down? Tell him Mahlorie is here."

"How do you know Dyson?" his dad asks.

"We met online," I lie.

"When?"

My shoulders shrug. "I don't know. A couple months ago. Why?"

They don't reply. At least I see where he gets it from. "Look, he told me to come here, to his house, and he'd be waiting for me outside on the front lawn, which he's obviously not. I wouldn't be here if he hadn't told me to come. So, if you could please—"

"Little girl, this isn't funny at all," his dad says, a faint Alabama accent lingers.

His mom starts to cry.

Am I in *The Twilight Zone*? This whole family is crazy or schizophrenic or something.

"He's homeschooled, spends time writing poetry, got in a bad car accident three years ago, and had a metal plate put in his head." They still stare at me like I've got the plague. "He's in a wheelchair." Still no reaction. I huff my frustration. "You guys own a hunting cabin in the woods. He spent summers there." I choose not to tell them how their cabin's now a charred ruin in the center of those woods. "Look, I know I'm a mess. It's been a long night and I'm trying to see your son in person to tell him something. Then I'm gone. I promise, you'll never see me again."

His mother still cries.

His father puts his arm around her frail shoulders. "Dyson's not here," his dad says.

It's as if lightning struck me again. My hairs

stand on end. "What do you mean he's not here?"

"I don't know why you'd make up a story like you did, but—"

"I didn't make it up. I was talking to him a few minutes ago before I got here."

"That's not possible," his dad answers.

"Well it happened. For some reason, I started hearing your son in my head and now I finally find him and he's refusing to see me."

"Is that true?" his mom whimpers. "Can you really hear him?"

"Of course not, Patti. She can't hear him. Don't play into the delusion."

"Delusion? Why don't you go ask him yourself?

He'll tell you."

Dyson's dad is the one who cries now. His mother takes my hand and barely whispers, "We can't, dear. Dyson's no longer here."

Lightheaded. "What? Where is he?"

"The hospital. He's been there ever since the accident." My heart drops to my feet. "Slipped into a coma and he never left." Darkness cataracts my vision. "He has no brain waves." World teeters like a top about to fall. "Dyson can't talk, honey. There's no way you've been hearing from him."

And my world goes black.

▫▫ PROOF ▫▫

I awaken in Dyson's living room, on a floral couch with itchy cushions. The walls are tinted pink and ornaments decorate high tables, fixtures, and oversized pots. Fake vines stream across the high plant shelf. Others fill in the gaps behind the furniture. The house is massive and expensive with old-fashioned decor. What was it like for Dyson to grow up here? Did he sit on this couch that scratches like sandpaper against my skin?

But I may never know. Dyson's in a coma. The reality floods my brain. A coma? It can't be possible. Why would he be able to talk to me? Why would the Universe bring us together if we could never truly be together? The unfairness of it all weighs heavy on me. How can I love someone who isn't really there?

Dyson's parents sit across from me on the matching love seat.

"Are you okay, dear?" his mom asks.

I am not okay. I feel no pain. Emptiness. Numbness.

"What's your name again?"

"Mahlorie Moore."

"I'm sorry to have to bring you such terrible news about Dyson's condition. We've dealt with it for a very long time, and it still hurts as badly as the first day." She's choked up.

"I don't mean to be disrespectful, but I don't believe this. It's too much." I face her. "Why would I be able to talk to your son if he's already gone?"

"When you say 'talk' what exactly do you mean?" his dad asks. He's broad-shouldered and beneath the wear from age, I can see the remnants of strong features and a square jawline.

Like Dyson.

"It's hard to explain." *These are his parents, Mahlorie. You have to trust them.* I take in and let out a big breath. "A few months ago, I was nearly struck by lightning…or maybe I was. Who knows? It's not important. Then, I don't know when exactly, but I was in class forced to answer a math problem that not even Newton could figure out, and I hear the answer in my head. Loud and clear. And I'm actually afraid to write it because that would mean I admitted I could hear the voice, you know?

"But the voice insisted I write it, so I did. And he started to freak out because I could hear him, like I was the first person he'd talked to in forever, which I probably was…now that I know the real situation. He told me to say his name out loud and wouldn't let up, so I screamed it out and he heard me. We could hear each other, this boy with a metal plate in his head from a car accident and me, a girl with a mouth full of braces who'd been struck by lightning."

His parents exchange a glance. Disbelief? Awe? Fear? I really can't tell, so I continue. "We think somehow the lightning must have put my braces and his plate on the same frequency, to allow us to hear each other." I face his dad. "He has your eyes, and I recognize you both from the pictures on the mantle in the cabin. Don't freak out. Dyson led me there one night, he rescued me, actually. He saved my life." Tears pool in my eyes. "He's the most amazing and…and…wonderful person I've ever known. I've risked everything to find him, to see him in person. To know he really, truly exists. To be with him."

I fall silent, and we stare at each other. I know his parents don't believe me, but there's no way I could make all that stuff up. They have to believe me. There's a reason we were brought together. I can't have him out of my grasp forever. I can't.

"This is ridiculous." His dad stands, paces, stares from me to the ceiling, before he says, "You know this isn't possible, don't you?"

I go to answer him, but he stops me.

"You also know too much for it not to be possible."

We are all quiet, except Dyson's mom who's sobbing softly.

"I know it's hard to understand," I say. "But we, Dyson and I, believe there has to be a reason why we can talk to each other. We didn't have enough time to figure it out."

It's quiet for so long, I don't know if I should get up, let myself out, and never look back. Instead, I sit stoic, lost in thoughts of my disappearance into Dad's trick or Mom's plotline.

Gaze fixed out the window, his dad says, "There's nothing that can be done, Mahlorie. It took Dyson's mother and I a long while to realize there wasn't anything we could do to bring back our son. But it's something we have to accept. Even you." He faces me, and my tears blur his image. "You couldn't be talking to my son. The boy is brain dead, and even if he did wake up, he'd be—"

"He's not brain dead!" I jump to my feet, cheeks flush with heat. "He writes the most beautiful poetry and has these thoughts about life and literature and love. I talk with him. I know him. No way he's not in there. He needs help to find his way out."

"What did he say was the reason?" his mom's soft voice chimes in.

"The reason?"

"That you can hear each other? Why does he think you communicate?"

I half-smile. "Something important. For a purpose that was bigger than us meeting…" My voice trails. This whole situation is ridiculous. Have I fallen down the rabbit hole? Have I lost my mind?

His mom stands, leaves the room, and returns with a document, which she clutches to her chest. "We've been hopeful Dyson would pull through, but with the doctor's belief that he no longer produces any brain waves, we agreed to…we need the doctor to sign off and…"

"We've decided to let him go in peace," his dad says.

My head is about to explode. "No. You'll kill him! Dyson's still in there! You can't pull the plug. You can't do that."

"Stop it," his mom begs. "You don't understand."

"No, *you* don't understand. Your son is alive. He's not brain dead."

His dad chortles. "Why would we take the word of a girl who's broken into our cabin and shown up on our doorstep to tell us she speaks to our son through her mind, over the doctor who's been with him since the beginning?"

"Because I love him." I'm on my feet. "And I

won't let you take him from me." I bolt to the door. Adrenaline drives me.

"How do we know you're telling the truth?" his mom asks, the paper—Dyson's death order—in her balled fists, as if it will protect her conscience if she follows through with its instructions.

"Because I am. How else would I know him? Why else would I be here?"

"Is he with you now?" his dad asks calmly.

Both his mother and I look at him. "What?" I ask.

"Is my son speaking to you, in your head, at this moment? Can he hear us?"

"No," I reply, defeated.

"Then how can we take your word for it?"

I don't have an answer. Facts points against me. I don't understand any of this. *Dyson, where are you?* But I know where he is, unconscious on a hospital bed with a metal plate in his head that needs to be adjusted so our frequency can connect again.

Oh, my God. That's it!

As I open the door, I say, "Take me to the hospital and I'll show you."

⌑⌑ THE DOOR ⌑⌑

Will miracles never cease? Not only does Dyson come back to me this morning, but I get a text from Shai while I'm in the Hertz's car:

I'm awake.

My fingers fly across my phone:

OMG! You're ok? I miss u!!!!

She types back:

Where r u?

I wipe a tear and reply:

Headed 2 hospital. He's there...

We pull in the lot, park, and enter through the glass doors. Shai texts back:

Dyson?

What happened? He ok????

It's too much to explain. 5 min out.

2 much 2 type.

We check in and ride the elevator to the pediatric wing. Shai doesn't text back. I tell Dyson's parents what happened to Shai to release nervous energy. When the door opens, I excuse myself to pop in and check on her, grateful for the stall, while they wait outside her room.

I'm so relieved she's back. I need to see her. "Hey," she greets me, her voice barely audible.

"Shai." I rush to her bedside and give her a huge hug. "I'm so glad to see you. I've been so worried. You okay?"

"They want to keep me here a little longer. Run tests. Then, I need a facial and something to wear besides paper dresses. Really not a great look for me." We share a small laugh. "Plus, the cell service in here is horrible. It comes and goes for no reason and it's driving me crazy. I'm trying to catch up on my shows and the network keeps freezing, then I lose the connection completely. Mal, you've got to get me out of here." She smiles her confident smile and we touch our foreheads together.

"I love you," I say.

"I love you too. So, what's going on with Dyson. He's here? On this floor?" She stares at my dirty face and hair for the first time. "Why are you such a mess?"

"Long story. I'll tell you later, I promise, but his parents are outside."

"You've met his parents?"

"It's complicated. He told me where he lived, and I went to his house, but he was here."

Shai gives me her look. "I've known you practically my whole life, and I have never seen you care for a boy or do anything remotely crazy for a boy. I don't know what it is about this one, but you're smitten. So, he's gotta be a god or something to have caught your heart."

I smile.

"I have that in Lucas. It's weird. I wasn't looking for it—real love—but now that it's here, I don't think I could live without it. Without him. Thank you for giving me his message."

"You're welcome." I kiss Shai on the cheek. I

know exactly what she means. "Be right back," I say as I head to the door. There's so much to tell her, but it'll have to wait. I'm glad she's back.

Outside her room, I follow Dyson's parents down the long hallway that leads to the window I escaped to after Shai's accident. And then it hits me. The couple I overheard...the boy in the coma....

I was this close to Dyson and didn't even know it.

We're at his door and my mouth goes dry. My legs wobble and I don't know if I can walk. Machines blip and bleep his vitals in the dark room. Then, I see him, propped up in bed with tubes down his throat and wires attached to his arms, head, and chest. I gasp, not ready for what I see. I force my leaden legs across the linoleum until I'm at his bedside. His lungs are forced up and down mechanically. He looks so peaceful. So fragile. So helpless.

"Dyson?" I whisper.

His eyelids flutter.

His mother cries.

"Mahlorie?" he says in my head, though his lips don't move. *"Where are you? I thought you were passing the clubhouse?"*

"I was." I gulp down pain. "I went to your house."

"I don't understand. How'd I miss you? I'm in the yard right now waiting. Why can't I see you?"

How do you break the illusion of reality to someone who lives in a dream? What words can convey the truth to Dyson that what appears to be his existence is a fabrication?

Why me?

With a deep breath, I say, "Because I'm not there anymore."

"I see that. What happened? Why'd you go?" His voice has changed, disappointment colors his tone.

"I had to leave."

"How come?"

"I couldn't stay," I barely whisper.

"Why? Where'd you have to go? I thought we were finally gonna meet?"

"I had to get to the hospital." My tears splash on his arm, roll onto his sheets.

"Is it Shai? Is she okay?"

"Yeah...she's fine. They're gonna run some tests, but then she should go home."

"I don't understand. Then why'd you have to run out to get to the hospital?" His arm twitches.

Was it from my tear? Did he feel it? His parents stand across from me on the other side of the bed. I speak out loud to him, which is weird, because they only hear my side of the conversation.

"Mal? You there?"

"I'm here."

"At the hospital."

"Yup."

"Why? What aren't you telling me?"

"I, uh...I came here...to see you."

He's quiet. In person, I swear he'd have taken a step back if he could. *"To see me?"*

"That's right." I wipe my tears, though twice as many replace them.

He laughs. *"What are you talking about? I'm in my front yard. Why would you think I was at the hospital? Where are you, really?"*

"I already told you. I'm at the hospital."

"To see me."

"To see you."

"This is crazy."

The monitors blip in response to his elevated heartbeat. His parent's eyes widen.

"Do you remember," I ask, "why you said we were able to hear each other talk?"

"Because the Universe wanted us to meet."

"But do you remember why?"

"I don't want to talk about this."

"You said it was bigger than us, remember? You said there was a reason, and you weren't afraid of it. Well, now I know why. And I'm not afraid either."

His pulse creeps higher, hands and eyelids twitch.

"I told you not to come looking for me," he says angrily. *"Why'd you go trying to find me, Mahlorie?"*

"Your accident...you never left the hospital..."

"Shut up."

My heart aches, steals my breath. "You fell into a coma...your parents were ready to let you go, to pull the plug, and—"

"I said shut up!"

"That's why I can hear you, don't you see? To prove to them that you're still in there. That you're still the same. And there's hope that you can find your way out of this, Dyson. I'm here with them, in your room. I'm right next to you."

"Shut. Up!"

I slide my hand on his. "Can you feel your hand in mine?"

"No. You're a liar and I wish I'd never met you."

My voice is low as I say, "I don't believe you."

"I don't care. I don't believe you. How could you do this to me?"

"Dyson, I love you. I need you."

"Get out of my head and don't ever come back."

"What?"

"Go away!"

He cries, whimpers in my head, and those tears stream from the corners of his eyes, down his cheeks.

His mom gasps.

His dad stares.

I tenderly reach for a tear and wipe it away with my fingertip.

"I'm holding your tear," I tell him. "And I'll hold every single one for the rest of your life. Open your eyes and wake up."

"I can't," he says.

"Yes, you can. You absolutely can. Try."

A silent pause lapses into a minute. I'm about to speak when he says, *"I've been trying, you know...to wake up. I didn't realize that's what I was doing. I meant it when I said I felt like I only talked when you showed up."*

"Well, they're gonna take you away from me if you don't wake up and show them that you're still in there. They're going to let you go."

"They can't. My parents would never forgive themselves."

"Then wake up!"

"I can't wake up! Are you listening? I don't know how to get out of this. I didn't even know I was here until you told me. This is bigger than me, Mahlorie. It's bigger than you. I can't make myself..."

"I know you can do this. I believe in you. I believe in us. Don't give up, Dyson. Follow my voice and let me lead you, like you led me through the water

18

to your cabin."

He cries, sobs. *"Will you do me a favor?"*

"Anything."

"Tell my mother, the sun only sets so we can start over tomorrow."

I look at his mom and say, "Dyson says to tell you that the sun only sets so you can start over tomorrow."

Her lips tremble into silent wails that fall upon her son's still body.

Dyson's dad cries too. "She's told Dyson that every night since he was a little boy. It's how she got him to not be afraid of the dark." He wipes his nose. "Can you tell my son that I love him? So much. We both do, and we miss him..." He, too, collapses in pain.

"Dyson," I sputter. "Your parents love you and they miss you. They want you to come home. We all want you to come back."

"Do you remember my poem?" His voice is the eye of a storm. *"Dead ends stretch to dark corners with no beginning..."*

"Dyson, wake up."

"Each time I think I've reached you, your hem is all I find, hugs the next branch."

His heart races, way too high.

"...this labyrinth is my prison..."

Nurses stream in, push me back, yank his parents away. His mom screams.

"...Not because I can't find the end..."

His pulse plummets into silence.

"...but because when I do, I know you'll be gone."

Flatline.

My heart is broken. They try to revive him.

I slide down the wall. My hands cover my face.

"It was always you, Mahlorie. The reason. I love you and I'll miss you forever."

I'm a ragdoll crumpled on the floor in a pool of my own tears. "Don't leave me."

"You were my greatest moment," he says. His body jerks from the electric paddles that shock his heart.

"Thank you for leading me to the door."

His voice disappears. Static fills my ears.

Radio silence. Gone.

⊡⊡ NEW ⊡⊡

Shai's discharged several days later, and her mom drives us back to the house. I'll stay with them until my parents come home.

Numb. Broken. Raw.

Powered down.

Rain falls heavy, sorrow from the powers that be, that mourn my loss.

Shai grabs my hand and smiles. I smile back the best I can. She's changed through this. We both have. It will be different between us. Our scars bind us. My time with Dyson separates my life into two parts: the world before him and this world without him. He taught me who I am. The girl who was afraid of everything is gone. And he showed me what love really is. For those gifts, I can never repay him.

A few weeks later, I receive a letter from his mother. It will be the last time we ever speak, but her words will stay with me, in a box filled with memories that I will never throw away.

Dear Mahlorie,

It is with conflicted emotion that I pen this letter. After three years, my only son has been laid to rest. And though the pain is at times unbearable, I know it will subside.

I wanted to thank you for being a part of Dyson's life and for allowing my husband and I our final words with him, something we never thought we'd have. Thank you for showing us Dyson was still there. I never would've forgiven myself if we'd followed through while Dyson had a chance of returning to us. For this, I am forever in your debt.

Whatever forces brought you two together gave us our son back and took him on life's terms. Thank you for your gift of comfort. If there's ever anything you need, please know that we are always here for you.

Sincerely,
Patricia Dottie Hertz

It's funny how life changes you. For me, I learned what love truly is. You can't seek it in a bottle, like my chemistry teacher tried. Or hide it in different colored rooms like my English teacher taught. And it's more than a sleight of hand or a perfectly constructed paragraph.

It's imperfect. It's flawed.

It's Shai with a guy who loves her and who I believe she truly loves in return.

As I figure out who I am, I can love and be loved. That's okay. There are people out there who don't care about popularity or clothes or trends, who want to make a difference in the world. I can find them now because I'm out of my own way. It's my dad, who doesn't pretend problems away like they're a magic trick anymore. And my mom who listened to my entire story about Dyson and didn't take notes to use it in her next manuscript.

Then there's me, Mahlorie Moore, a girl who was struck by lightning and found the love of her life. And I'm not sad that Dyson's gone. Sure, I miss him. I miss what we could have been. But that never was our reality. We lived in a place that doesn't exist and for the briefest moment, the universe allowed us to be together. To know each other in an impossibility. That's what I hold onto. That's what has changed me. What is love? It's different for everyone. For me, it's a lightning strike and a boy who rescued me from inside my head, which became the beginning of the rest of my life.

▫▫ THE END ▫▫

THANKS TO YOU!

Thank you to my incredible list of Beta Readers who caught plot holes, fixed my grammar, and made all kinds of corrections!

Christine Aurigema
Kelly Dwenger
Jessica, Julia, and Olivia Paolicelli
Jason, Elaine, and Sarah Irizarry
Karen Dibbern
Elaine Ewertz
Jenny Beiser
Bill and Nancy Allen

ooooo

And a huge thank you to Joshua Menendez of *Just Josh Draws* for the incredible cover art! You captured Mahlorie perfectly.

Philip Benjamin of *Benjamin Studios*, thank you for another stellar cover design job!

FROM THE AUTHOR

Metal Mouth was one of my fastest books to write, and Mahlorie literally poured onto the page. She was so easy to create and I am so connected to her. The story idea came to me in a dream. I woke up laughing out loud because in my dream, a girl who wore braces got struck by lightning and could suddenly hear a strange boy's voice in her head. I thought the idea was so crazy and I couldn't imagine what that would feel like. So I had to write the book.

There are a few serious issues that are brought up in *Metal Mouth*. The most obvious is safety. Both nature and its creatures can kill you, so please be safe, especially in storms and around alligators. The more serious issues involve alcohol and driving. It's not a joke. I personally have had friends killed by drunk drivers. Never get in a car with someone who's been drinking. The other topic in this book that I want to address is physical contact that isn't welcome. You have the right to tell anyone, "No," if they make you feel uncomfortable, or hurt you. No girl or boy should ever get in your space without your permission. Problems can escalate very quickly and turn dangerous. Always reach out to a trusted adult and let them know if.

Thanks for being a fan and for reading my books!

jaihie
engle

If you enjoyed this book, please take a moment to review it.

Follow the author on all social media platforms @jaimieengleauthor

Jaimie loves working with students through school visits & writing groups. Visit JaimieEngle.com for details.

ABOUT THE AUTHOR

Jaimie Engle writes books filled with wonder and discovery for t(w)eens. Before publishing her first novel, Jaimie danced at the Aloha Bowl halftime show, was an alien on Sea Quest, and modeled bikinis for Reef Brazil. When not writing, Jaimie is on Tik Tok or cosplaying at a comic convention.

Learn more at www.JaimieEngle.com.

Made in the USA
Columbia, SC
05 June 2022